BACHELOR BID

City slicker Benedict Laverton is billed as top prize at the Coolumbarup Bachelors' Ball. To escape the ordeal, he persuades one of the organizers, Rosy Scott, into bidding for him with his own money. But Rosy gets carried away, bidding a cool $10,000 . . . When she goes on stage to claim her man, Rosy not only has to face Benedict's stunned disbelief, she has to kiss him too — a kiss which is spectacular enough to convince her that getting involved with Benedict will end in disaster . . .

SARAH EVANS

BACHELOR BID

Complete and Unabridged

LINFORD
Leicester

First published in Great Britain

First Linford Edition
published 2014

A catalogue record for this book is available
from the British Library.

ISBN 978–1–4448–1862–8

Published by
F. A. Thorpe (Publishing)
Anstey, Leicestershire

Set by Words & Graphics Ltd.
Anstey, Leicestershire
Printed and bound in Great Britain by
T. J. International Ltd., Padstow, Cornwall

This book is printed on acid-free paper

Dedicated to my family.

1

The sharks were circling for the kill. Scarlet slick lips shrilly discussed the talent. Sharp eyes, over bright with cheap champagne, boldly scrutinized the goods.

And he was the goods.

Benedict vowed to wring his mother's neck at the earliest opportunity. Because this was a farce of significant magnitude. In a few moments, he'd be served up like a slab of meat and sold to the highest bidder.

He scanned the sea of hungry female predators. In normal circumstances he liked women — loved them. In normal circumstances he'd be chatting up the most beautiful lady in the joint. In normal circumstances, he wouldn't be here! But these weren't normal circumstances. There were far too many women in one, confined place. And they could smell blood. His blood! They were baying like a pack of foxhounds. Terrific.

'Whatever possessed you to volunteer me for this Hicksville Bachelors' Ball?' Benedict growled at his mother when she finally descended on his table in a flurry of expensive midnight blue tulle. 'You could have asked me first. Or at least have warned me.'

'And why would I done that? You're so stuffy, darling, you would have said no,' said Martha Laverton, laughing. 'Anyway, you'll enjoy yourself once you relax.' She paused a moment, her eyes twinkling. 'The trouble is, Ben, you've forgotten how to party and have fun.'

'I have a perfectly adequate social life, thank you.'

'I don't consider business dinners and corporate golf matches adequate. They're a poor substitute for the real thing. You're still a relatively young man, you know. You should learn to loosen up and enjoy yourself more. Hours stuck in your office, bean counting, have atrophied your soul.'

'I don't bean count. I deal with high

2

finance,' replied Benedict, deliberately ignoring the jibe about his age.

Martha gave a mischievous smile. 'If you say so, darling. I'll go see how soon you're on.'

Benedict watched her glide away, still an elegant figure at seventy. She flicked a casual hand in recognition of someone and bestowed warm smiles on others.

It still surprised him that his high society, widowed mother had moved from the comfort and sophistication of Perth to this small town in rural oblivion. Okay, so she'd always gone on about living the good life and being part of a community after years traveling the world with his father. But Benedict hadn't actually expected her to do it, Personally, he couldn't see the appeal of living in the sticks, away from the bright city lights. What on earth was there to do in the country, other than organize awful fund-raising events?

He grimaced. Well, his mother was certainly in the thick of that particular activity.

He should have been suspicious when she'd insisted he visit her this weekend. She'd lured him with promises of plentiful wine, mouth-watering food, and lots of pampering.

He still hadn't realized what his mother had planned when, as soon as he'd arrived at her beautiful rustic home, she had spun a sob story about how she'd bought tickets for a ball and her escort had dropped out at the last minute. He'd simply swallowed the bait and allowed himself to be rigged out in his Dad's old tuxedo — though why she still had it he didn't know. She'd got rid of all his father's other clothes. The possibility that the suit had been hired or bought specially for him didn't even cross Benedict's mind — until later.

Then he'd been led to the ball like a lamb to slaughter. How could he have been so gullible?

He'd only begun to feel twitchy when he realized the charity ball was a bachelor auction: a thinly disguised meat market where single men were auctioned off for a fistful of dollars.

He'd almost blown a fuse when he discovered *he* was the bachelor with top billing.

Raucous laughter from a nearby table made Benedict wince. A gaggle of less than gorgeous girls was viewing the merchandise and loudly, unsubtly, discussing his finer points. Resolutely, he turned his back on the giggling group and stared into his wineglass.

'I feel like a prize bull in a ring,' he complained to his mother a few moments later, when she'd returned from backstage.

She laughed and patted his cheek. 'Don't worry, son. It'll soon be over.'

'Not soon enough.'

'I'm sure you've endured worse things.'

'Now I wonder why root canal work immediately springs to mind?'

'Oh, Benedict, you do go on. Just remember to be nice to whoever wins you,' said Martha in a tone she'd used often during his childhood. 'You have a duty to do.'

'Don't I know it!' Benedict dreaded to think which over-painted woman, decked in psychedelic bad taste, would buy the right to his company. 'I can't believe I have to spend the rest of the ball with them and then have the dubious pleasure of escorting them to an 'intimate' dinner tomorrow night. Who dreams up these tortures?' He shuddered.

'It won't be that bad and it's all for a good cause,' said Martha. 'Now, I have to go and help backstage for a while. Good luck. Or is it break a leg?' She went away laughing, which only made him feel worse.

Benedict scowled. What had he done to deserve such a fate? He stuck a finger down his collar and tugged. It felt tight. It felt like a noose.

There had to be a way out of this. A way in which his mother wouldn't lose face among her new set of friends, but would let him off the butcher's hook.

Benedict scanned the hall for inspiration. His gaze skidded over the neighbouring table and then swung back, his attention snagged by a solitary figure.

Hmm. A sparrow of a woman in a drab coffee-colored dress. He'd met her earlier for a very brief moment. He couldn't remember her name, he'd been too busy reeling from the shock of his bachelor billing status to pay attention, but she was one of the organizers. The hairy-chinned female sergeant major in charge of operations had clapped him painfully on the back and told him to ask whatever-her-name-was if he needed anything during the course of the evening.

Well, he did.

An escape.

Urgently.

★ ★ ★

Rosy slumped wearily in the chair. Her head throbbed with a humdinger of a headache. Helping run the ball was always a stressful experience and it

7

never got any easier. This was her third year and, she vowed, it was definitely her last on the committee. She'd done her time. Now it was up to someone else to be bullied by the ball mafiosa.

She slipped her aching feet out of her high strappy shoes and wriggled her toes. Bliss. She closed her tired eyes. Heaven. The buzz of the ball receded. She allowed her breathing to slow and deepen. She just needed a few moments to recharge her batteries. No one would notice.

A hand landed heavily on her shoulder, jolting Rosy out of her delicious intermission.

'Wah!'

Something was thrust in front of her face. It looked awfully like a check.

'What the-?' Rosy shook her head to clear the shades of sleep. It was a check.

'Five thousand should cover it,' a man's voice rumbled close to her ear. The hairs on the back of Rosy's neck shot skywards and she reared back.

'Five thou-?' She shoved the check

away from her face so she could get the thing in focus. Yup, it clearly stated five thousand dollars. She whisked her head sideways to eyeball the tall man towering over her. It was the suave celebrity bachelor. He was a real coup for their little ball or so some thought. Personally, she reckoned all the hype and fuss over Benedict Laverton was totally overblown. At the end of the day, he was just a man in a fancy suit.

'I can see it's a check. What's it for?' she asked, puzzled.

The man flexed his jaw as if he was having difficulty forming the words. 'It's for the auction.'

'Yes, but Mr. Laverton, you don't have to pay anything. You're the one up for sale. It's the women who do the buying.' She patted him kindly on the arm as she squinted up at him. Surely Laverton of all people would understand how an auction worked? He was a business genius, for goodness sake.

She watched his straight dark brows snap together and his mouth thin to a sour, dour line. Now why did she suddenly get the uncomfortable feeling she wouldn't like what came next?

'It's the women I'm worried about. I want you to bid for me.'

'Me?' Rosy squawked. 'Me bid for you? But why?' Surely he hadn't taken a shine to her when they'd met briefly at the beginning of the evening? She hadn't thought she'd made much of an impression, if at all. And she seriously doubted he fancied her in her shapeless, charity shop dress held together with a battalion of safety pins.

Though, what if he did?

The audacious idea sent a blush roaring across her cheeks. Benedict Laverton might just be a man, but he had been voted one of the country's most eligible bachelors. A successful, rich, and supposedly ruthless financial wizard, if the popular press was to be believed. It would be a heady experience to be singled out by someone of his dangerous caliber.

And he hadn't been put off by her

awful frock. Good grief. It proved there was no accounting for taste. Although, for the zillionth time that night Rosy wished her son Josh hadn't upended his orange juice over her one decent dress, forcing her to wear this dismal brown thing.

'I want you to do it just for appearances' sake,' Benedict said. 'Then we don't have to bother about tomorrow night. We can end this nightmarish scam here and now. No one would be any wiser. The charity will get its money and I can disappear.'

Pop! Rosy's bubble burst. Her blush rolled away on a wave of humiliation. Stupid me, Rosy mentally kicked herself. Of course he wasn't attracted to a worn out, washed-up, old scarecrow like her.

Anyway, she couldn't do it. Wouldn't do it. What with the boys and all.

'I can't bid for you.'

'Why not, for heavens sake?'

'Because I can't. What would everyone say?'

'It's an auction! You're expected to bid!'

'Yes, but not me. I don't bid. People will think . . . ' What would they think? That she'd lost her marbles? That she'd robbed the local bank? Or was cashing in on her child support big time?

'I don't give a snap what people think! I don't want to be sacrificed to those piranhas.' He waved at the full hall. Rosy followed the sweep of his hand. He had a point. There were some pretty formidable bidders out there. But he was being such a wimp. Why?

'You're not scared, are you?' she goaded, a sudden, husky chuckle escaping before she could stop it.

'No! Of course I'm not scared.' He hesitated a beat then confessed, 'I'm absolutely terrified!'

Rosy gave an unladylike snort.

Benedict groaned. 'It's all very well for you to laugh,' he said bitterly. 'You're not the one in the firing line.'

'True. How about I find someone else who can do the bidding and won't expect your undivided attention? I'm sure I can rustle up someone.'

Maybe.

'Please. I'll be forever in your debt.'

'Okay.' She frowned and tried to hit on someone, anyone, but her concentration wasn't helped by the enthusiastic cheering of the crowd. Then all of a sudden the Master of Ceremonies declared the auction open and called for Benedict to come to the stage.

'Oh great, here comes the press gang,' said Benedict and he slapped his hands together in supplication, his dark gray eyes beseeching. 'I'm relying on you. Please! It's too late to find anyone else. You'll have to bid for me,' he said as the main organizer, Deirdre Bott, and two other women came to frog march him to the stage. 'Don't let me down!'

'I can't do it!' she squeaked. But he had gone. Rosy looked at the check Benedict had dropped on the table. Five thousand. He must be pretty desperate to wriggle off the hook. Not that she blamed him. Some of the women would easily eat him for breakfast and still be hungry.

She raised her eyes to the stage where the MC was jovially thumping the reluctant celebrity bachelor on the back and playing up to the audience. She stifled a giggle. Top billing at the auction was an extremely dubious honor. She was surprised Benedict Laverton had agreed to be in it in the first place, though not that he'd tried to renege. In her experience, it was typical of a man to make a promise and then break it.

Rosy was tempted to leave him to his fate. Benedict Laverton was no pussycat in need of rescuing, not like some of the young, fresh-faced bachelors who'd been 'persuaded' to participate by Deirdre and her cronies.

No, he was a hard-headed businessman used to cutting a swathe through life regardless of the consequences, if the gossip columns were anything to go by.

But he had asked for her help. Hmm.

14

Rosy sighed. She supposed she could bid for him. It would be cruel not to, when he was expecting her support. Unfortunately though, it would set tongues wagging. The community was used to her nun-like existence since her husband Steve had shot through. She was one of the last people anyone would expect to bid at this auction. And most would know she couldn't afford to throw away huge sums of money. As it was, she could barely pay the household bills.

Still . . .

'Do I have a bid?' The auctioneer began his patter, fielding bids from the excited audience.

Rosy nibbled an unpolished finger-nail. She'd never bid at the auction before. Had never paid attention to that part of the evening. She'd always been out back preparing supper or weaving between the tables collecting dirty glasses. So when would be the best time to enter the fray? Now? Later? Never?

Never would be tempting!

Benedict stared stonily ahead. This was awful. The screaming, squealing women bidding for him were scary. And that dragon lady Bott was beaming as the bids escalated. Benedict almost cracked his back teeth he was clenching his jaw so hard. When was the sparrow going to start bidding? She'd better do so quickly, because the alternative was terrifying.

'Five hundred from Joanna. Do I hear more? Six from Nina. Eight hundred from Joanna, one thousand from Nina,' cried the auctioneer. The bids rolled in and peaked at two thousand. 'Do I hear more?' asked the auctioneer.

There was a charged silence. Benedict swallowed hard. The bidding had stopped with Joanna Pennington's offer. He'd met her earlier. She was one of the town's movers and shakers and she smiled at him now like a well-satisfied cat who knew it was going to be served the canary,

16

complete with gravy and sage stuffing.

A surge of frustration rammed through him. The sparrow wasn't going to bid! She was going to abandon him to the mercies of a man-eating woman.

'Two thousand once . . . Two thousand twice . . . ' intoned the auctioneer.

'Two and a half.' Rosy's voice floated low and husky from the back of the hall. Heads bobbed about to see who had made the late bid.

'Is that you, Rosy Scott?' The auctioneer's voice boomed over the PA.

'Yes, it's me.'

Benedict couldn't see her, but Rosy's voice wobbled as if she was nervous.

'Okay, my dear.' There was a definite tone of disbelief in the MC's voice. 'Do I have another bid? Three. Thank you, Joanna. You're not going to be outdone, then. Ha, ha! Rosy? Another bid?'

'Three and a half,' said Rosy, and Benedict was dimly aware of the surprise washing through the hall.

'Where does a girl like Rosy Scott get that sort of money, that's what I want

17

to know,' whispered Deirdre Bott to someone behind Benedict's back.

What sort of girl was Rosy Scott, then, Benedict mused. Until now, he hadn't given her character much thought. She'd just been a convenient escape route.

'It's shameless. She should use the money for the kiddies, poor little things, not men,' went on Mrs. Bott.

So, this Rosy had children. Was that why she'd been so reluctant to bid? Maybe her husband was a jealous man? Now that would really cap a good night, to have a raging, green-eyed spouse added to the proceedings.

'I always thought she wasn't what she seemed. No wonder Steve left her.'

Benedict ground his teeth. Nice people! He had obviously dropped the poor girl right in it. But it was too late to do anything about it now. He'd apologize to her later, once this fiasco was over.

'Rosy?' said the auctioneer. Benedict switched his attention back to the bidding.

'Four and a half.'

Atta girl. Keep going, Benedict urged her silently. He prayed Ms. Nympho Pennington would give up soon. The thought of spending an evening with her unnerved even him. There was a definite raptorial glint in her eye.

'Five thousand!' declared the MC. 'Well done, Joanna.'

★ ★ ★

Rosy was sweating buckets. She could feel beads of moisture trickling between her breasts. Her mouth, though, was paradoxically dry. What should she do? Should she carry on spending Benedict Laverton's money past the five thousand mark or not? In the rush, they hadn't made a contingency plan and from this distance there was no way to tell what he wanted her to do.

She stood on tiptoe, trying to get a clearer view. Darn, but it was useless. She needed a pair of high-powered binoculars just to see the stage, let alone read Bachelor Laverton's expression. This was terrible. She'd have to rely on instinct.

And gall!

'Rosy? Do you bid?' said the MC.

The people in the hall seemed to hold their collective breath. The auctioneer raised his voice. 'Five thousand once, five thousand twice, five-'

Suddenly, Rosy was zinging from an overdose of adrenaline. She couldn't, wouldn't back down now, not after coming this far. She was committed to the eyeballs. A red haze clouded her vision.

She managed to unstick her tongue from the roof of her mouth. Her first attempt to speak came out a croak and she hurriedly cleared her throat and yelled 'Ten!' at the top of her voice.

Her blood fizzed with her own audacity. The buzz of power was addictive. The shocked disbelief on everyone's face added to the thrill.

Yes! She felt like punching the air like a goal scoring footballer.

Yahoo!

2

'Ten thousand! Going once!' There was dead silence.

'Going twice!' Dead, dead silence.

'Going three times!' Total, spine-tingling silence.

'Rosy Scott, after that stupendous bid, he's all yours,' said the MC. 'Congratulations! Let's give them a big round of applause everyone.'

The hall erupted into uproarious clapping and cheering. Rosy stood completely still in the sudden furor. It was like being in the eye of a storm. Everything was calm and silent on the inside, while chaos reigned on the out.

Her blood fizzed and popped, then settled to a dull roar as the adrenaline oozed away. The red haze dispersed. Sanity re-asserted itself.

Had she just bid ten thousand dollars?

Good grief, what had she done?

'Come up on stage and claim your prize, Rosy,' shouted the MC over the clamor. Rosy wobbled forward on unsteady legs. The ground seemed to undulate beneath her feet, impeding her progress. The walls wavered, the ceiling rippled. People opened and shut their mouths. She couldn't hear a thing they said because of the roaring in her head.

Ten flipping thousand! She couldn't believe it. What if Benedict Laverton didn't honor the extra five thousand? She couldn't hold it against him. She'd done a terrible, terrible thing pledging all that money without his consent. She'd have to increase the mortgage on the house. Take out a loan. Beg!

Steady girl, she slammed down on the panic. First things first. She had to brazen out the next awful few minutes and pray she wouldn't be exposed as a fraud. Otherwise, she didn't know if she could handle the ensuing fall-out of being ribbed by everyone in town and incurring Deirdre Bott's wrath.

22

And then, of course, there was Benedict Laverton to consider.

'Claim your prize, my dear,' the MC laughed with heartiness. 'Give the lady a kiss, Mr. Laverton. That's the etiquette around here. She's certainly earned it.' The crowd hollered its approval.

Someone pushed Rosy toward Benedict and she suffered the briefest of salutes on her overheated cheek. Phew, thank goodness that was over. It wasn't so bad. She raised wary eyes to glance at Benedict. Would he be angry about her outrageous bid?

Oh, Yes!

Livid.

His eyes were stormy gray and turbulent, with a few lightning sparks just for good measure.

Well, tough! What did he expect, dropping her in it like that? He was the one who'd wanted her to bid for him. None of this was her fault. Not really.

Well, okay, maybe a bit, by bidding all that money.

'Come, come, young people,' the MC crooned boisterously. 'The lady just promised a record-breaking ten thousand dollars for the choicest bachelor in town. I think she deserves a better kiss than that. We're all adults here, you know!'

The crowd roared with laughter and Benedict imagined another thousand ways of crucifying his mother for getting him into this. She owed him big time. And so did this woman standing in front of him, cheeks flushed, and staring at him reproachfully with large, puppy-dog brown eyes.

He couldn't believe she'd pledged away a cool ten thousand dollars of his money. Ten thousand! It was a small fortune. He felt only slightly mollified when he saw Joanna Pennington's furious face. At least he'd been spared that ghastly fate.

The crowd was still making a din, chanting for Benedict and Rosy to kiss. 'Kiss! Kiss! Kiss!' the people yelled.

So, they wanted him to kiss the little

sparrow in her ill-fitting sackcloth that smelled ever-so-faintly of mothballs? Okay, he would. Never let it be said that Benedict Laverton didn't do his duty.

He'd also kiss her to exact his pound of flesh for the whopping bid she'd made on his behalf.

Reaching down, he pulled Rosy roughly into his arms and unerringly swooped towards her mouth, watching her eyes snap wide in surprise.

'No,' she said on a breathless gasp.

'Yes,' he countered, his lips almost touching hers. 'You generously spent ten grand of my money. The least you can do is give as generously of your mouth.'

Her protest was swallowed, as his bold lips clamped over hers and began to move with cool deliberation. He blocked out the noise of the audience and concentrated fully on the woman's lips beneath his. He'd give her the kiss they demanded — long, hot, and hard.

And he'd take it too — long, hot, and hard!

It was good in theory, but somewhere

during the long, hot, and hard, Benedict lost his way. He gradually realized her lips were unexpectedly soft and sweet. They tasted of sun-warmed wine. Delicious. Intoxicating. He wondered about the rest of her mouth, but her lips remained forcibly together.

A frigid little sparrow? He'd see about that. After all, she'd cost him a packet. It was pay back time. He nipped her lips with his teeth, causing her to gasp again, and he slid smoothly, determinedly under her guard.

Mmm.

To the backdrop of catcalls, hand clapping, and foot stomping, Benedict teased his tongue along her teeth, stroked the sensitive inner lip, before diving in to tangle with her tongue.

Mmm, mmm, yes. She sure did taste sweet.

★　★　★

Rosy struggled to avoid his invasion of her mouth, but there was little she could do. His tongue tangled with hers and she felt a sudden surge of heat shoot straight through her body. Her heart rammed against her ribcage and she was momentarily paralyzed.

Their tongues silently dueled and Rosy thought she would melt on the spot there was so much fire running through her veins.

Rosy's hands clenched into fists on the lapels of Benedict's expensive jacket. She shoved against him. He had to stop. Now. She pushed harder. Benedict responded by jack-knifing her backwards and Rosy whimpered as her hips were pinned intimately against his. There was no mistaking he was as aroused as she was.

Any second now, Rosy reckoned, she would die of embarrassment, if asphyxiation didn't kill her first. The agile gymnastics of his mouth were robbing her of oxygen. She was lightheaded and weak-kneed. It had been an eternity since she'd been kissed so thoroughly.

No! Correction. She had never been

kissed so completely. Damn Laverton. He'd short-circuited her nervous system and every atom whirled out of control, going faster by the second.

She hoped she had an inner trip switch somewhere in her body, otherwise she was in danger of blowing a fuse. Failing that, Deirdre Bott would have to break out the fire extinguisher or call out the volunteer fire brigade.

★ ★ ★

As Benedict tilted Rosy backwards, he experienced an acute, high-voltage burst to his system. Passion bloomed and tightened hard in his gut, sending his pulses rocketing, making him light-headed. Fire met fire and the heat intensified. It was amazing.

He ignored his small inner voice of reason which whispered this had got to stop, for both their sakes. Why should it? It was good. It felt right to have this fiery beauty burning in his arms, consuming him with her unexpected heat.

But the voice kept on until it couldn't be ignored. Benedict had to admit there would be hell to pay if this passion grew any hotter!

Slowly, reluctantly, Benedict began to ease up, drawing Rosy upright. He kissed her a little while longer, just for the pure pleasure of it and then slowly, reluctantly ended it, enjoying one last nibble on her full, throbbing lips.

He lifted his eyes to meld with hers, expecting them to be soft, warm, tender, and passionate, to match her mouth.

But they weren't.

They were passionate, all right, but with fiery fury. But how could she be angry after such a fantastic kiss? It had been pure heaven. But there was no mistaking it. She was spitting mad.

In spite of her anger, Benedict kept his arm coiled tightly around Rosy's slim waist. He told himself it was to steady her trembling body, but it was more to enjoy the feel of her. And he kept his arm there as they followed

Deirdre Bott off stage so the auction could continue.

Deirdre looked Rosy up and down. 'Well, Rosy, what a surprise,' she said forthrightly. 'Who would have thought you, of all people, would bid for our top bachelor? So, how are you going to pay? Cash? Credit card? Check?'

It was laughable! Rosy tried to squash a sudden surge of hysteria. Here she was with zilch to her name and she was expected to fork out a whopping ten thousand dollars for the dubious honor of spending some intimate moments with Stud Laverton.

She didn't want any intimate moments with him if the public one was anything to go by.

She was still steaming from his kiss, even though she had vainly tried to resist it with every atom of sensibility. How dare he take such advantage and cause her heart to back flip a thousand times a second! She was a respectable mother of two, not some wanton witch with an exhibitionist streak.

Hadn't that been the sort of crass public display Laverton had said he'd wanted to avoid? He'd been mad to kiss her like that. Totally.

But how good it had felt.

Rosy almost groaned aloud at her traitorous inner voice. But it had felt good. It had been tender, sweet, inviting, and she'd been in danger of a total shut down of her nervous system.

But how could she have responded like that to someone who'd indicated he didn't fancy her? How would she react if he kissed her and decided he did find her attractive?

Her toes curled at her own answer.

And so did her lip — in derision — at both herself and Benedict. She shouldn't have responded at all. He shouldn't have taken liberties when she was the one helping him out of an awkward situation!

'Rosy?' Deirdre was impatiently waiting for her answer. 'Cash, credit card or check?'

Except for Laverton's check that

she'd crumpled in her hand during their spectacularly passionate and public kiss, she had nothing but a few dollars and a handful of IOUs in the children's moneyboxes. Her bank account was terminally ill and her credit card was stretched to the max.

'Rosy?'

'Sorry, Deirdre.' Rosy nervously twiddled a strand of hair that had escaped from its loose knot, thanks to Benedict Laverton's questing fingers! 'Look, I'll have to, er, settle up tomorrow. I didn't, er, expect to bid.' She dared not admit it had all been a set up. Not now that they had come this far. 'As you know, I don't usually participate in the auction side of the evening.'

'But she was driven to do so tonight. As soon as we met, Rosy was bowled over by my charm,' Benedict smoothly cut in. 'And couldn't resist me.' His arm tightened around Rosy's waist. 'Isn't that right, darling?' he added with such bone-melting warmth Rosy almost expired on the spot.

Darling? He was calling her darling? Rosy inwardly panicked. What was going on here? Why the sudden charm? She wished she could expose Benedict Laverton's scam, but ten thousand dollars for the hospital auxiliary's charity fund was at stake.

And her own reputation.

She couldn't do it.

'I was amazed, I must admit,' remarked Deirdre. 'I didn't think you would have had any spare cash to spend on any of our bachelors. I would never have guessed.'

Rosy clung to her smile with difficulty. Her fingers convulsed around the check. She'd like nothing better than to chuck in the whole ridiculous charade.

She felt a tremor run through the body of her captor. So he thought all this was funny, did he? Hah, so was this. Rosy deftly stepped sideways and landed, heel first, on one polished black shoe.

Benedict yelped, but hid it with a

coughing fit, hugging Rosy closer to his side. She struggled to break free, but Benedict's hand remained firmly on her hip.

'Come and see me tomorrow,' Deirdre's brisk, no-nonsense tone cut through Rosy's preoccupation with her stuttering heartbeat. 'I must return to the auction. Enjoy the rest of the evening, Mr. Laverton, and, of course, you too Rosy. It goes without saying that you'll be relieved from tonight's kitchen duties. We can't have you neglecting our celebrity bachelor, now can we.'

More panic whisked through Rosy.

Goodness, she didn't want to be left alone with this dead-sexy man. Cleaning up leftovers and washing dirty plates was infinitely preferable. She would volunteer to clean up single-handedly, even if it took her until daybreak, if she thought it would solve her predicament.

'It's all right, Deirdre, I can still do my stint,' she said hastily.

'Rosy, sweetheart, after splashing out a cool ten thousand dollars, you must get your full value for your money,' said Benedict.

Did she imagine the silky menace underlying those words? It did nothing to dispel her rapid heartbeat. He wasn't going to let her get away with spending his money. What did he mean by full value for her money? Rosy broke out in a cold sweat. He wasn't going to kiss her again, was he? Anyway, hadn't he paid through the nose to avoid having to escort a local girl? She began to relax again. Of course he had. He was simply keeping up the act. He was good, too. He'd even had her fooled.

'Let's go have a drink.' His warm breath feathered across her bare shoulder and she gave an involuntary shiver that reached to the tip of her toes.

'Good idea,' she croaked and tried to wriggle away from his possessive hold. She failed. He tugged her closer, tucking her neatly under his arm as though she was a well-loved teddy bear.

Again, she attempted to break free, but she only succeeded in dislodging one of her thin shoulder straps. It skimmed dangerously down her arm. Before Rosy could haul it up, Benedict was there, his fingers brushed against her suddenly sensitized skin. He deftly hitched the rogue strap back in place with a dexterity that begged the question of how he'd acquired the skill.

Rosy could have coped if he had left things there. But he didn't. Oh no. The next moment his dark head dipped forward and warm lips whispered a kiss where his fingers had been.

Rosy's stomach contracted sharply. Her breath caught in her throat. The shivers zipped back up from her tippy-toes. Good grief, he couldn't take liberties like that all evening. She'd be a gibbering, quivering wreck.

Who was she fooling? She already was.

Cracking down on her somersaulting nerves, Rosy swatted him away. 'Leave me alone!' She inwardly cringed at the sudden huskiness of her voice. Where was her backbone when she needed it most? That's right, melted by that scorching kiss of Laverton's! 'Leave me alone or I'll re-auction you,' she hissed.

'You wouldn't dare,' Benedict grinned unrepentantly, whisked up her hand and brought it to his lips. 'You're too soft hearted.'

'Not me, mate. I'm tough as old boots.' She tugged at her hand. It did no good. It remained firmly entwined with his. She gave him her best glower. It didn't appear to cower him. In fact, annoyingly, his grin broadened.

'I don't believe you. You wouldn't have helped me out if you were an old harridan.' He turned her hand over and kissed her warm palm, letting his lips play over it invitingly, while his teeth grazed the soft swell of flesh by her thumb.

Hot, acute desire ripped through her. She couldn't suppress it. This was worse than running a marathon. At least then she knew where the finish line was. With this infuriating man, there was no telling where it would lead.

Oh come on Rosy, she railed herself. It wouldn't lead anywhere unless she wanted it to. She was no inexperienced virgin. If she didn't want a man, she didn't have to play the game.

And she didn't want a man — any man. Been there, done that, end of story. It was time to assert herself before she got in too deep. She hauled her hand away, successfully this time.

'Stop mauling me,' she snapped, flicking her hand behind her back and scrubbing away his kisses on her dress.

'But you enjoy it.' His slate gray eyes twinkled with humor and challenged her to deny it.

'No I don't. I hate it,' she said with bold defiance, but crossed her tingling fingers like her boys did when they told a white lie.

Benedict grinned. 'I don't believe you. Your skin sings to my touch, Rosy Scott. Look how you shiver.' His index finger skittered across her shoulder with rose petal softness. A rash of goose-bumps mushroomed in its wake.

Rosy spluttered ineffectually. This man was trouble. She must get a grip. She didn't want to be off-balance by this attractive stranger with his killer touch. She liked being in control, had to be in control for her peace of mind and her boys' future.

'See,' he said as Rosy shivered again.

'I'm cold,' she protested.

'Ah, is that what it is? Sorry, but I beg to disagree.'

'Are you calling me a liar?' Rosy pursed her lips.

'Let's just say you're in denial.' Rosy opened and shut her mouth, amazed by his gall. But before she could think of a retort, Benedict went smoothly on. 'What I think you need, sweetheart, is a relaxing glass of wine after all this . . . excitement. It'll calm you down.'

'What I need,' muttered Rosy, low under her breath so he couldn't hear, 'is to get out of here fast.'

3

Benedict glanced down at the muttering woman and suppressed a chuckle. She looked as if she was going to explode on the spot. Her cheeks were streaked angry red, her turbulent umber eyes were alight with golden fire, her bee-stung cupid lips were drawn into a formidable line, masking the sensual lushness he'd discovered there. She radiated total enmity.

'My table is this way,' he said, putting his hand on Rosy's arm to guide her through the crowded hall.

'I know where it is,' she snapped, shaking off his hand and stalked ahead of him, her spine rigid with hostility.

'I see. So I wasn't telling whoppers to Deirdre Bott. You were attracted to me from the start or you wouldn't have bothered to work out where I was sitting.' Benedict's voice shook with laughter.

'When Hell sells ice-cream, mate. I know where your table is because I reserved it for you. It was one of my duties as a member of the ball committee.'

'You don't have to play coy with me, Rosy. I fully understand and I'm flattered.'

Her usual humor deserted her, Rosy spun around on her heel to face him. Outrage exploded in her eyes. She jabbed a finger hard into the middle of his chest and said, 'Don't be, you'll be bitterly disappointed.'

'Let me be the judge of that, Ms. Scott,' he returned easily, catching her hand and holding it against his crisp, snow-white shirt over his beating heart.

Rosy gasped and quickly yanked her hand from his warm grasp. She almost ran toward Benedict's table as if pursued by a pack of rabid dogs.

Benedict followed her at a more leisurely pace, his mind whirring at the direction the evening had taken. He could hardly credit that, until half an hour ago, he'd been itching to escape from the ball. Now that had all changed. His interest was snagged and he was immensely looking forward to ruffling this little sparrow's feathers.

Benedict had to admit he'd been completely mistaken about the young woman. His first impression had been one of dowdiness. It had been an easy error to make. Her sludge-brown sack of a dress deserved to be burnt. It hid a body with curves in all the right places. He knew. He'd felt them under the thin fabric when he'd hauled her close for their very public kiss.

And what a kiss!

He couldn't wait to kiss her again. Just the thought made his blood heat and his heart pound faster. But he wouldn't kiss her yet. He'd have to wait for that treat, for a time when she was less hostile. The delay didn't worry him in the slightest. Benedict thrived on challenges and he reckoned he had a big one on his hands with Rosy.

Benedict ruefully acknowledged it

had been the longest time since a woman had so effectively fired his interest. These past few months, he'd been up to his neck in work and hadn't had the time or inclination to date seriously. While he hadn't been totally devoid of female company, they'd only been half-hearted affairs. Benedict decided any affair with Rosy would be far from half-hearted and that attracted him even more.

Rosy continued to glower as Benedict pulled out a chair for her.

'Comfortable?' he inquired solicitously.

'Yes, thank you.' She plopped into it, acting more like a sulky teenager than a mature woman and he couldn't resist goading her more by brushing his fingers lightly across her shoulders as he helped her settle. It was satisfying to see the shiver and flush of her skin. 'But not if you do that!' she huffed.

Benedict laughed and shook his head. He was very, very tempted to drop another kiss on her shoulder to see what further chaos he'd cause, but he didn't. She was a bundle of nerves already. He didn't want to alienate her until he'd explored this surprisingly potent chemistry between them.

This contradictory woman had piqued his interest and not only because she had coolly bid 10K of his money. Was it because of her looks? Her brown dress was awful, but that was just superficial. The rest of Rosy Scott was rather delicious — her silky hair and satin soft skin, her curvy, firm body. He liked her smile, even if it hadn't yet been bestowed on him. It was sultry yet whimsical and powerful enough to blast a hole through the ozone layer.

She was one attractive woman who'd caught him on the hop after a dating drought. Why not enjoy it while it lasted? After all, he'd paid ten grand for the privilege.

'What would you like to drink?' he asked Rosy.

She stared at him for a moment, weighing him he suspected, or trying to find a loophole to get out of the situation. 'A red wine,' she said finally, expelling a long sigh.

'You don't have to sound so defeated,' he said after giving their order to a waiter and zeroing his attention back on Rosy. 'You could just enjoy yourself.'

'That would be novel.'

Rosy twiddled a strand of loosened hair and worried about the enormous bid that had to be paid the next day. She was extremely concerned she'd be morally liable to pay half of it. Five thousand was a huge amount. She'd never had that much spare cash. She always operated on a shoestring. Even if she did have that sort of extra loot, it would be criminal to spend so much money on a so-called date when she had so many other urgent things to spend it on for the boys. What was she going to do? There was only one way to find out. Confront the cause of her problem.

'How are we going to settle this fiasco?' she asked Benedict bluntly.

'Which bit are you calling a fiasco?'

'You know, the bid. It's an awful lot of money. I still can't believe I did that.'

'Nor me,' said Benedict dryly.

'I'm sorry.'

'Don't be. I'll write a check to cover it. No sweat. Anyway, there are bound to be some compensating factors.'

'Like?' she asked doubtfully. She certainly couldn't think of any.

'I can think of several possibilities.'

Uh-oh! Judging by his expression, she didn't dare inquire further.

Their drinks were set on the table and Benedict raised his glass to her. 'Here's looking at you, kid.'

Rosy silently saluted him with her wine and took the tiniest of sips. She wanted to keep a clear head. She'd need all her wits about her to survive the evening with Bachelor Laverton and his so called possibilities. He looked far too smug for her liking.

There was a round of applause as another bachelor bit the dust and then the MC announced there would be a short break in the proceedings for some dancing.

'That's just what we need,' said Benedict, rising from his chair and scooping up Rosy's hand. He tugged her to her feet. 'Let's dance.'

'Oh, no!'

'Oh, yes! It won't be that bad. Regard it as one of the compensating factors. Anyway, I'm considered quite a reasonable dancer. I took classes as a kid.'

'I wouldn't have had you down as the kind of kid to dance.' Rosy was momentarily curious and then could have kicked herself for showing any interest.

'I wasn't. It was on the curriculum. I promise not to tread on your toes unless strictly necessary.'

'That's the least of my worries.'

'Why?'

Because I'll be in your arms and I don't think I can handle it after that kiss!

'You don't want to know.' Well, he might, but no way was she going to admit how dangerous she found him. He'd already rattled her enough for one night.

'But I do want to know.'

She involuntarily shivered. 'Well I'm not going to tell you,' she said and was relieved when the band struck up a jazzy number. At least she could keep her distance and avoid touching him.

Some hope.

Benedict pulled her on to the dance floor and spun her into his arms.

'What are you doing? This is a fast dance,' protested Rosy, trying to push against his rock-hard chest without much luck.

'I'm not going to jig around like some teenager. I want to dance cheek-to-cheek.'

Eek!

'You have a problem with that?'

'Yes! I don't do cheek-to-cheek.'

'So this is a night of firsts for you. You said you hadn't bid before either.'

'True, but I didn't say I hadn't danced cheek-to-cheek before. I said I didn't do it. At least not with you.'

'I'm offended.'

'Oh dear.'

'You don't sound very sincere.'

'I'm not.'

'At least you're honest.'

'I am. So I'll tell you now, I'm not enjoying this, so let's go and sit down.'

'No, let's carry on dancing.' Benedict drew her closer. Rosy could feel the heat radiating from him. She radiated a high temperature too. This was not good. In fact, this was very bad. It was giving her the jitters.

Benedict settled his hand just above the swell of her hips. She twisted her arm backwards and planted his hand further up on her waist, which was in her opinion a slightly safer zone. Slightly being the operative word. It was still dangerous.

'Spoilsport,' he chuckled as he rested his chin against her hair and drew her even closer, so now her breasts were squashed flat and his heat had fused with hers.

'Always. It's my middle name.'

'I'd change it by deed poll if I were you or you'll never have fun.' His hand inched back down to her bottom.

'Mr. Laverton!'

'But it's more comfortable resting there. And speaking of names, I think it's high time you began calling me Benedict, especially now that we're more intimately acquainted.' He snuggled her closer in spite of her resistance.

'Behave yourself!' Perturbed by his actions and inwardly vowing never to call him by his first name, Rosy cast eyes over the other dancers. Nobody else was smooching. This was so unfair and so embarrassing. No wonder her blood pressure felt high and her heart was zipping along at a hundred miles per hour. She tipped her head back to eyeball her partner. He looked dark and dreamy.

And dangerously sexy!

'I think we should sit down. I'm beginning to feel very hot.'

'So am I,' he smiled. 'So let's keep dancing.'

Rosy hoped she had mistaken that sultry glint in his dark gray eyes. Hoped he didn't mean what she thought he meant. Because if he did, she was in deep trouble.

'Really, I do need to cool off. The hall is so stuffy.'

'I suppose it is.' An arrested expression came into his eyes. 'We could go outside. Now there's an interesting idea.'

Hot panic immediately attacked Rosy's nerve endings. 'No way!' she squeaked. In her sudden consternation, she missed a dance step and landed heavily on Benedict's foot.

'Ouch!'

'Sorry. But no way will I go outside with you.'

'Why not? It's a perfectly logical idea. It's much cooler outside than in here. And we could admire the stars.'

'It would be suicidal!'

'That's a bit strong.'

'Never. I learned back in high school that sneaking out of a dance didn't

51

mean you were going star gazing.'

'Really?' Benedict grinned. 'So what did it mean? What did you do?'

Rosy gave him what she hoped was a withering look and didn't deign to answer him. Some things were best left unsaid.

'Coward.'

'Every time. Please, I really, really want to sit down.'

And get out of your arms so I can breath easily again and put a halt to the slow burn in the pit of my stomach.

'Okay.' He reluctantly pulled away, but then the band changed its tempo and started to play a slow, bluesy song. The haunting sound of a saxophone spiraled around the closely packed hall, swirling between the dancing couples. Benedict immediately dragged Rosy back against his body. 'I love this song,' he murmured into her hair. 'You wouldn't deprive me of the exquisite enjoyment of dancing to it, would you?'

'Yes.'

'Goodness, you're a hard woman. Be kind.'

'Give me one good reason.'

'You spent ten thousand dollars of my money.'

Now that hit below the belt.

Rosy nibbled her lip. He did have a point, but golly, she really didn't want to shuffle around the hall trying not to melt in his arms. Her nerves were already shot to smithereens.

'This is the last dance,' she finally said, 'and then we go back to the table.'

It turned out to be the last dance before the auction recommenced. Benedict led Rosy to their seats, helping her into her chair again like the perfect gentleman she was sure he wasn't.

'So tell me about yourself?' Benedict said.

'There's nothing to tell.'

'Well, I know you have kids and no husband,' he stated.

'How did you know that?'

'I have my sources. So how long have you been on your own?'

'None of your business.'

'It's no big deal, Rosy. I'd just like to

know a little more about you.' Like why you're so illogically hostile towards me and yet you shiver with suppressed passion in my arms.

'My personal life doesn't concern you.'

'I'm trying to make conversation here.'

'No need.'

'So let's get this straight — we can't talk and we can't dance. So, what can we do?'

'Suffer.'

'Great. I pick the one man-hating woman in the hall to bid for me. What absolute luck.'

'You didn't pick me. You took potluck in your panic to weasel out of the evening. I did suggest I find somebody else to bid for you,' Rosy pointed out.

'So now it's all my fault?'

'Yes.'

'Excellent. Okay, I take full blame. Why can't you chill out and just enjoy yourself? The evening will go much quicker and will be a great deal more pleasant if you do. Unless, of course, you want to sit and scowl at me for the next few hours.'

'I don't mean to scowl at you. Sorry.'

'That's a start. Good. We can build on that.' He sat back in his chair and grinned. Finally, he was making progress.

'All right. But, if you don't mind, I'd like to freshen up,' she said. She put a hand up to her loosened hair and Benedict's grin expanded as he realized he was to blame for its dishevelment.

'Go ahead. Take your time. I'm not going anywhere.'

He watched her zigzag her way past the tables of merry makers, glad he was making headway with the prickly Rose. Suddenly, the weekend looked very promising.

Minutes ticked away. Her glass of Merlot sat untouched. Benedict half-heartedly tuned into the antics of the auction and every so often glanced over to the restrooms. There was no sign of Rosy. He looked at his watch. When he said take her time, he hadn't meant a week! She'd been gone forever. Was she trying to re-group after their sizzling encounter? Just thinking about her mouth under his was sufficient to send his blood zinging.

By the time he'd finished his glass of wine, Benedict realized that Rosy Scott had stood him up.

4

'So did you kiss anyone, Mum?'

The Spanish Inquisition was underway over the cereal bowls. Rosy could have done without the third degree as she ate her muesli. She was tired and preoccupied. But her sons were curious, avidly so. Usually she found their rampant inquisitiveness appealing. Cute, even.

But not this morning.

'So did you?'

'Yes,' she said shortly.

Both boys gasped. Too late she realized she should have lied. Being a stickler for honesty had its drawbacks. Joshua's eyes widened considerably at her candid confession. She could just about hear his brain humming.

'On the cheek?'

'Yes.' Rosy munched on stoically. She prayed five-year-old Josh would stop there, though she didn't hold out much hope. Josh had the tenacity of a pit bull. But so did Rosy and she had no intention of discussing last night's smooch. 'Come on, stop dawdling,' she said with guilt-fuelled impatience.

Josh dutifully shoved a spoon of milk-sodden Wheaties into his mouth and was silent for all of thirty seconds. He swallowed and said, 'On the lips?'

Rosy chewed until the muesli turned to cardboard. While she chewed, she wrestled with her conscience. She loathed lying, especially as her ex-husband had been so darned good at it. But if she lied and the boys heard about the farce at the ball, she'd find it harder to demand honesty of them later. With their father's track record, she couldn't afford to take that risk. She swallowed the cardboard.

'Hmm, yes. Now hurry up.'

'Oh gross!' Josh squealed in fascinated disgust. 'Does that mean you're getting married?'

Rosy choked on a rogue oat and began to cough. She took a swig of scalding tea that did little to help. 'No!' she managed to croak. 'Don't be ridiculous. Eat up.'

'But you said you only did that kissy stuff if you were getting married.'

'Sometimes! I meant sometimes. You don't always get married when you kiss.' Life couldn't be that simple, could it!

'But you said . . . '

'I know what I said, but sometimes it's a little more complicated than that.' She hoped that explanation would suffice and shut him up for a while.

It was an empty hope.

'But, Mum . . . '

'Josh!'

'I only wanted to know if it was nice.'

Rosy fought back a surge of heat. Nice? Not the word she'd have chosen to describe Benedict Laverton's hot kiss. But then she hadn't quite worked out how to describe it. Except it had packed a powerful punch and she wasn't going to share that with her sons.

'Was it, Mum?'

'For heavens sake, Josh, just get on with your breakfast.'

'Who'd you kiss?' Matthew, her older boy of seven, then asked.

Uh-oh, now the other son with a broadside question. Brilliant.

'Who, Mum?'

Rosy thought she could detect a note of panic in the boy's voice. She couldn't blame him. Last night's kissing made her feel downright panicked too, as had the dancing and the chit-chat, which was why she'd done the only sensible thing under the circumstances — she'd done a bunk from the ball. Just like Cinderella.

'Just someone,' she said and shoved a piece of buttered toast into Josh's mouth, so at least one of the children was quiet.

'But who?' Matt pursued.

Rosy sighed. She'd have to come clean, but she'd only give the barest of facts. 'Just one of the bachelors from the auction. No one you'd know.

Anyone for more toast?' Both boys shook their heads. But Rosy sprang from the table anyway and clattered about the sink to put an end to the awkward discussion.

It was a relief when the doorbell chimed. One of the boys' friends must have come around early, which was not an unusual occurrence on a Saturday morning.

Wiping her hands on her jeans and linking a strand of silky brown hair behind her ear, Rosy scooted along the hallway. On the way to answer the bell, she picked up a discarded red sock and an inside-out school jumper off the floor. She then opened the front door. Her cheery smile of welcome crashed down to her scuffed joggers, while her heart lurched painfully against her ribcage. Defensively, she clutched the sock and jumper to her thudding chest.

It wasn't one of the boys' friends standing on the doorstep. Oh no. It was the imposing figure of Benedict Laverton on her front porch.

And he didn't look happy.

'Rosy.'

'Mr. Laverton,' she croaked. It was all she was capable of after her lungs abruptly ceased to function.

The aloof, tuxedoed tycoon who had sent her pulses sky-rocketing with a kiss the night before was just as deadly in his casual black designer jeans and plain white shirt. All that understated wealth and power was totally intimidating.

Rosy shivered with trepidation. This was no Prince Charming searching for his Cinders with a glass slipper. This was more like the Big Bad Wolf hunting Red Riding Hood with his sharp teeth.

Was he going to be nasty about her sudden disappearance last night? He looked as if he might. His dark eyes were stormy gray, his black brows were drawn tight together, and his mouth was a rigid line.

There wasn't time to find out because small feet thundered down the bare-boarded hallway and two little heads poked out from either side of Rosy.

'Hello, who are you?' asked Joshua, who still had cereal encrusted around his mouth. Before Benedict could reply, the boy said, 'Are you the man Mummy kissed?'

'Josh!' Rosy scrunched her eyes shut for an agonized second and tried to put her hand over her son's mouth. 'Sorry, Mr. Laverton.'

'Are you?' insisted Josh.

'Well, yes,' said Benedict, obviously struggling with the knowledge that Rosy filled her children in on her night out. He shot her a wary look. 'I suppose I am.'

'Oh. So are you going to marry her then?' pressed Josh. 'Because Mum says you only kiss the person you're going to marry.'

'Marry!' Benedict echoed, as Rosy groaned. She wouldn't blame Benedict for feeling as if he'd been hit on the side of his head with a mallet. She was experiencing a similar stunning of the senses.

'Yes,' said Josh with the sweetest of innocence. He was totally unaware of the emotions he was creating in the two adults.

'Josh!' Rosy's whole body was cold with shock. She must stop him.

'It's okay, Mummy. I was only asking. You always say to ask if you need to know something and I want to know if . . . '

'Yes, yes, we heard you. But not now! Sorry,' Rosy muttered again to Benedict. She shot him a nervous look. His anger seemed to have evaporated. He looked absolutely poleaxed. Hardly surprising. It probably wasn't every day Benedict Laverton, bachelor extraordinaire, was confronted by a midget interrogator demanding to know his intentions towards his mum.

Up until this precise moment, Rosy had considered the comments that tripped out of the mouths of her sons as cute. Now she wasn't so sure. Gagging them suddenly held a great deal of appeal.

'Marry!' Benedict repeated, shaking his head from side to side as if trying to clear it.

'He doesn't actually mean it,' Rosy hastily soothed, attempting to minimize the damage.

'Yes I do,' contradicted the midget.

'No you don't and that's the last of it,' Rosy countered sharply. 'Sorry, Mr. Laverton.'

'Exactly why are you sorry?' asked Benedict. 'Because of your son's candid questions or because you ran out on me last night?' He raised his dark eyebrows inquiringly.

Rosy gave an awkward shrug. 'For both, I suppose. It was rude of me.'

'What else happened last night, Mummy?' asked Matt, with all the earnestness of a serious seven-year-old.

No way was Rosy going to furnish him with details! 'Back to your breakfast. Now! Quick smart.'

'But we've finished.'

'Go and get ready, then.'

'But, Mum!'

'Now! And take these with you.' She thrust the clothes into Matt's hands and pushed both boys in the direction of the kitchen. She spun back to Benedict. 'Sorry. Again.'

'Don't be.' He gave her an assessing look. 'Was it because of the children you didn't want to be involved in the bidding last night? And why you shot through later?'

Rosy flushed and tilted her chin challengingly. 'Yes. I had to get back for the babysitter.'

And I needed to put a chasm of sanity between us.

'I apologize if getting you to bid for me put you in a difficult situation. It wasn't intentional. I was being selfishly one-eyed about my own predicament.'

'Oh, I . . . ' That took the wind out of her sails. Rosy hadn't expected him to be so nice about it. His Big Bad Wolf image dissipated somewhat.

'Forgive me. Please.'

'Well, yes. And thank you for being so understanding,' said Rosy, even more surprised by his candor. Her attitude softened further towards him.

It was short-lived.

His next words made her instantly poker up again.

'But the fact remains, you spent a whole heap of my money last night and then left me high and dry. Imagine how I felt, being stood up by the sexiest woman at the ball after she'd bid a record amount of money for me.'

Sexiest woman? Her? Who was he trying to kid! She didn't want his empty compliments. But she'd try and placate him anyway and then perhaps he'd go away.

'I'm sorry,' she said and felt as if she was beginning to sound like one of the boys' nasty battery-operated toys that had malfunctioned. 'I thought it was best to leave. The evening was almost over and we had agreed that you'd write a new check for Deirdre, so there was nothing more to stay for, really, you know . . . '

Benedict frowned darkly as Rosy's

lame excuses petered out.

Okay, so there had been at least another two hours of dancing, they hadn't quite agreed on when the check was to be signed, sealed and delivered, and it had really been her duty to stay and keep the celebrity bachelor company. But these were minor points. Weren't they?

'Okay, so I'm very sorry.' There she went again. 'Sorry, sorry, sorry.' Rosy reckoned Matt's parrot couldn't have done it better.

Benedict stared at her for one long moment. 'So am I,' he said and hesitated a heartbeat. 'I was hoping to get to know you better. And I wanted to kiss you again.'

Whoosh! Color streaked across Rosy's cheeks. That kiss! It was going to haunt her. It already did! She'd been trying to forget it for the past few hours, denying its impact on her mind, body, and soul. She'd tossed and turned in bed during the few hours she spent there, making a total tangle of her sheets as her body had remembered the affect of that kiss.

And he wanted to kiss her again? No way!

'Look Mr. Laverton . . . '

'Benedict, remember.'

'Mr. Laverton!' her steely tone was one her boys would have recognized immediately as her don't-mess-with-me variety. 'I'm a single mother. I don't go around kissing strange men, paid for or otherwise.'

'But you did. Me.'

'That was under exceptional circumstances,' she blustered. *Leave it alone, Laverton. Leave ME alone!*

'It was. But I can't see any reason why those circumstances aren't still valid.'

'I can! I let you off the hook last night by bidding for you. I didn't have to, you know. I did it out of the kindness of my heart. But the ball is over. It's all finished. There's no more obligation, apart you writing that wretched check. We've both done our bit and now you're free to go. And I'm free to get on with my life without you

69

dogging my steps.'

'That's it? You just want me to walk away?' He sounded incredulous. Offended, even. But Rosy decided that was his problem, not hers.

'Yup. It's not hard, one foot in front of the other. You have a difficulty with that?'

Benedict dragged a distracted hand through his hair. 'Yeah!' he said. 'When a woman spends a tidy sum of my money, I do expect something in return.'

She wasn't seriously suggesting terminating their far too brief liaison? Good grief, he wanted to kiss her again. Even now, with her belligerent stance — hands on sassy, slim hips, legs akimbo, and a fierce light in her sultry golden-brown eyes — he wanted to kiss her.

'I wasn't the one on the market,' Rosy pointed out. He could hear the ice dripping from each word. 'You were. I was spending your money to save you from the clutches of Joanna Pennington and her cronies.'

70

Benedict had experienced an extremely lucky escape. He knew it. She knew it. Benedict inwardly shuddered as he remembered all too vividly the predatory gleam in Ms. Pennington's raptorial eyes.

'Quit while you're ahead, Laverton. Write your check for the auction committee and that will be the end of it.'

End of it? No! Rosy Scott had no idea how devastating and addictive her kisses were, Benedict realized. She hadn't the slightest inkling of the effect she'd had on him. How could he forget the feel of her luscious, heated body, fragrant with her womanly scent, straining against him? And what about the soft sweetness of her lips under his? No, he couldn't walk away. He couldn't forget. He wanted more than just a memory. He wanted a replay.

'You can't wriggle away from your responsibilities that easily,' he said. 'I want something to show for my money.'

You! Though he didn't dare say it, because her eyes had darkened to molten gold and her full, generous lips had thinned. She looked as if she was going to explode at any moment.

'I'm not for sale!'

'But you owe me.'

'I don't owe you a brass monkey. Last night you simply wanted me to bid for you. I did. Against my better judgment I might add. So that's it. End of story.'

'But that was last night.'

'Nothing's changed.'

'Everything has.'

Rosy threw up her hands. 'Like what?'

'I kissed you.'

Goodness, there he went again. Stuck on a kiss. She fervently wished he'd stop referring to it. It was deeply embarrassing. 'It was just a kiss, for heavens' sake. Everyone kisses. We all do it all the time.'

'You kiss everyone like that?' He sounded as mad as a cut snake.

'No, of course not. I don't kiss just anyone! Look, it's none of your business whom I kiss or how.' What type of woman did he think she was? 'Just duck out of my life. Permanently.'

Benedict scowled. 'It's not that simple, Rosy. What about the dinner tonight?'

'Dinner?'

'Yes. The dinner that's part of the bachelor package. The package you paid a cool ten thousand for with my money.' Benedict crossed his arms across the wide expanse of his impressive chest and leaned against the porch wall. Rosy eyed him with deep down panic. He gave her the impression he wasn't going to go away and he was prepared to do battle.

She gulped. Her salivary glands began to work overtime and it wasn't the thought of eating with Benedict, which was a bad enough scenario. No, it was the idea of him kissing her, which was even worse.

'No way,' she said. Benedict scowled more and Rosy had the distinct impression she was missing something here. Why would he want to take her out to dinner after all the shenanigans to avoid taking out a local girl? What nefarious designs was Benedict Laverton harboring?

She was determined not to find out.

'But it was part of the deal, an intimate dinner for two. I read it in the auction posters and Sergeant Major Bott confirmed it.'

Rosy's lips twitched at his reference to Deirdre, but she refused to be sidetracked by his humor. She did not want to be seduced by his charm. She'd already got into hot water by allowing him to persuade her into bidding for him and he hadn't been very charming then. So what would he be like if he was really trying to be nice to her? She felt a tremor of panic. At least, she thought it was panic. No, she definitely wouldn't listen to him again.

'You pledged all that money so you wouldn't have to suffer the ignoble fate of the gourmet tete-a-tete. Or have you forgotten?'

'No, that was my original aim. But

that was before I kissed you. Now everything has changed.'

'Nothing has changed, Mr. Laverton!' How could he say such shocking things? That kiss changed absolutely nothing, except her heart rate and that wasn't an issue in this discussion. Her sanity was at stake here. She must remain focused.

'Benedict! The name's Benedict! Now what's the big deal about sharing dinner with me? You've got to eat. So have I. And there will be a perfectly good meal waiting for us tonight at the . . . the . . . ' he frowned, grappling to remember the name of the restaurant.

'Laughing Duck,' Rosy supplied dryly.

'Yes, that's the one. Do you know it?'

'Mr. Laverton, we only have one restaurant in this town. The Laughing Duck is it.'

'Oh.' The town was smaller than he'd first supposed. 'I could always take you to a restaurant in another town if you don't want to eat there.'

'And hurt the Metcalfs' feelings? I wouldn't dare. They always host the post Bachelor Ball dinner.'

'So you will come with me tonight. Good.'

'I didn't say that!'

'No, but you did say we couldn't hurt the Metcalfs' feelings.' He grinned smugly and resisted the urge to lick his forefinger and mark an imaginary scoreboard.

'You don't even know the Metcalfs!'

'I'm willing to be guided by someone with superior local knowledge. So what time shall I pick you up? Seven thirty?'

'Fine,' she snapped, not bothering to conceal her bad grace. 'But I want the check now so there's no chance of further negotiation.'

'You drive a hard bargain, Rosy Scott.' Benedict smiled down into her eyes. They glittered with hostility. His gaze dropped to her full, kissable lips squashed together into a rigid, uncompromising line. He had the almost irresistible desire to kiss her bad temper away, smooth her frowning brow with butterfly soft caresses, slide his fingers through her hair and massage the tension away.

'The check, Laverton.' She tapped her foot with impatience, unaware of the direction of his thoughts.

'Ah,' Benedict quickly snapped to attention and dragged his checkbook from his back pocket. He slapped his hands over his other pockets. 'I don't seem to have a pen on me. May I borrow one?' He held his breath, hoping she would invite him in, maybe offer him a coffee. Anything, just so he could spend a little more time in her company.

Rosy stood there glaring at him. It was discouraging. No, it was downright deflating to his ego. Why was she so damn snitchy? He wasn't a bad bloke. Hadn't he just been billed as the star bachelor?

Rosy huffed and spun on her heel. 'You'd better come in.'

He didn't wait for a second invitation, but hopped over the threshold and followed Rosy as she stalked down the hallway. Benedict admired the view. She looked pretty spunky in her skin-tight blue jeans and equally tight black T-shirt. They suited her so much better than the ghastly brown sack she'd worn to the ball. Her long, silky hair was caught back in a swinging ponytail, free from the repressive pins of the previous night. Benedict itched to loosen the hair from its tie and watch it cascade about her shoulders. He was tempted to reach out and rediscover the enjoyment of its silky softness.

Rosy abruptly stopped and spun around. Benedict narrowly missed slamming into her.

'Pen.' She tossed it into the air and Benedict caught it mid flight. Her eyes shimmered with a challenge for a second before she set about clearing a space amid the breakfast clutter for him to write the check. She economically collected up jam-sticky plates and half-empty cups, noisily stacking them in the sink.

'Nice kitchen.' It was daffodil yellow

and airy. An array of childish art was pinned haphazardly on the walls and over the fridge.

'I didn't have you pegged as an interior design expert.' Her sarcastic tone nettled Benedict.

'I was being polite, making conversation.'

'You don't like it, then?'

'Yes. No. It's different. Not what I'm used to.' Off-balance, he glanced at Rosy. She was grinning. He'd been had. Hmm, he wasn't used to being teased, at least not since boarding school. He hadn't liked it then and he didn't know if he liked it now.

'Just write the check, Laverton, and while you do, I'll go and fetch the check you wrote last night so you can cancel it. After that, you can split.'

He scowled. What was the matter with the woman, anyway? Why the rush? How come she wanted him out? He filled in the new check and was signing it as Rosy breezed back into the kitchen. She slapped a crumpled piece of paper down in front of him.

'What's that?' he asked suspiciously.

'Your check.'

'Really?' He gingerly picked it up and straightened out the creases. There were a lot of them. Yes, it was his check all right, but it looked as though it had been through a meat grinder. 'What happened to it?'

Rosy hopped from one foot to the other. Benedict would have sworn that she actually squirmed.

'Well?' he asked.

'I was holding it when er . . . we were on stage.'

Benedict couldn't hold back his smile. 'You mean, when I kissed you on stage?'

'Something like that.' She squirmed some more and his smile widened. 'Okay, yes, when you kissed me. Satisfied? Now hurry up and go.'

'You expecting your boyfriend or something? You seem in a tearing hurry to get rid of me?'

'Yeah, the whole football team will

arrive any moment now.'

'Very funny.' There she went again — tease, tease, tease.

'Believe it.'

'I thought you said you didn't go kissing around.'

Rosy rolled her eyes. 'Who said anything about kissing? You're obsessed, Laverton.'

And with good reason. His eyes honed in on her cute cupid-bow mouth. Who wouldn't be obsessed when one had tasted her glorious honeyed sweetness? If only he could take her in his arms now and satisfy his hunger for her.

The sudden squeak of the fly screen door abruptly slammed the lid on Benedict's thoughts. A little voice piped up, 'Hi, Mrs. Scott.'

Rosy continued to hold Benedict's gaze while addressing the newcomer, 'Hi yourself, Sammy. How you doing?'

'Good.'

'So, you fit?'

'You betcha.'

'Excellent. Go on out the back and start warming up with the others. I'll be with you in a sec.' A glimmer of a smile flitted across her face. 'If you've quite finished, Mr. Laverton, I've got a team to coach.'

Benedict experienced an unnerving wave of relief. Not an adult football team, then. Phew! More like the under fives. He could handle that. He grinned, full of confidence once more. 'Like me to help? I used to be a pretty hot player in my day.'

'A fair few years ago, I'd say.' Her eyes traveled over him in rapid assessment, keeping her face bland so Benedict couldn't read her expression. Shame, he would have liked to know just what she was thinking.

'Twenty at least,' she jibed.

Actually, perhaps he didn't want to know.

'Not that many!' he protested.

'You've gone soft sitting behind a desk and pushing around bits of paper all day.'

'I keep in shape. Feel that.' He held up his arm and bunched it to emphasize the bicep. Even he had to admit, it looked impressive for a pen-pusher.

Rosy gave a snort and spun away, but not before he caught a flare of panic in her cute brown eyes. 'I believe you, Laverton. Put your equipment away. Purleese! If you're so keen on proving yourself, you'd better get out the back with the squad.'

Benedict slowly lowered his arm. A smile tugged the corner of his mouth. So she didn't want to touch him, eh? Not so immune to him as she'd like him to think. Hah! Watch out, Rosy Scott, I'm on your case!

He decided there and then that the romancing of Ms. Scott was top priority. Sure, it might necessitate a certain amount of delegating of his Perth business responsibilities so he could actually spend time around this feisty young woman, but delegation was long overdue. It was about time his under managers were given freedom to flex their management muscle.

It had been an age since Benedict put pleasure before business. Even his mother had voiced her opinion the previous night that he should relax more and have fun. And hadn't he dished out the same advice to Rosy only an hour or so later? As far as Benedict was concerned, relaxation and fun with Rosy would be of benefit to the both of them.

How altruistic he was.

Benedict chuckled.

Now all he had to do was convince Rosy to join in the fun. He squeaked open the fly screen door and joined Rosy and her motley group of boys in her big backyard.

5

Benedict lowered himself carefully into the steaming bath and winced. It wasn't only the scalding water causing him pain. Had Rosy Scott done it on purpose? Or was every training session that deadly?

The dog had been a definite menace, continually barking and tripping him up at every turn. He gritted his teeth as numerous cuts and grazes were cauterized by the hot water.

And those young boys had been a rabble of wildcats. No style. No technique. But sheer exuberant courage. Had he ever been so gung-ho in his youth? Probably not. He'd never nursed a death wish.

'There's some Radox in the cabinet if you want to soak,' Martha Laverton's muffled voice called from the other side of the bathroom door.

'A whisky would be better,' he hollered back.

'Too early in the day. Use the Radox.'

Benedict could hear her chuckling. Let her laugh. He'd get his own back one of these days. It was all her fault he felt so lousy. If she hadn't sacrificed him for the Bachelor Ball, he'd be spending his Saturday lunchtime at the latest oceanfront eatery with some undemanding, beautiful companion and the promise of a long, lazy afternoon. Instead, here he was with every muscle bruised and strained, and a dull ache in his belly from wanting Rosy Scott so much. Too much, damn her.

He found the Radox and poured half the packet into the bath, under the fully running taps. Whoosh! There was kick back of highly scented steam that made him gasp. Oof! The wretched stuff was rose-scented. Great, now he didn't only feel like death, but he smelled like the inside of a funeral parlor! But it was too late to do anything about it. He'd just have to reek of roses for the next few hours. He sloshed backwards to lie prone and determinedly shut his eyes. He would enjoy this small luxury regardless of Rosy Scott and his mother. He fully intended to be sparking on all fours by the time his seven thirty date arrived.

He moved his leg to twiddle with the hot tap and groaned aloud as his thigh and calf muscles complained. Rosy had been right. He'd gone soft. He'd have to invest more time at the gym if he wanted to keep up with Ms. Scott. And he fully intended to. Maybe he should take up jogging as well? But only if he was ever able to put one foot in front of the other without pain.

★　★　★

Rosy sang gustily under the shower. Needles of scalding water stung against her heated skin, washing away the sweat and grime of the morning's workout. She always felt invigorated after the two-hour training session and today's had gone particularly well. The boys were shaping up nicely.

She squirted a hefty dollop of strawberry shampoo into her hand and massaged it into her slick wet hair. She effortlessly hit a high note with more pizzazz than melody and wriggled her hips to the snazzy tune. She felt great!

It had been fun watching Benedict Laverton struggle to keep up with her youthful rag-tag squad. To give the bloke his due, he'd thrown himself enthusiastically into the game. If he came down a mite hard on occasion, he'd bounced back with surprising verve. He was fitter than she'd given him credit for, though she had detected him sloping along with a slight limp. And she'd caught him carefully rotating his shoulder after eye-balling the dirt when the dog had slipped his chain and joined the game. She had apologized through giggles, but she didn't know if he'd taken her seriously. He probably thought she'd let Henry loose on purpose.

At least the footy had diverted him from his kissing obsession. But for how long? There was still tonight to get through.

Rosy abruptly stopped singing. Tonight. What a shame she didn't have any spare cash to buy him off! She really, really, didn't want to go out to dinner with him.

Well, okay, so she did. She wasn't dead yet. She was just like the next woman. She wasn't immune to a hunky, handsome guy who showed some attention. Or a lot, in Benedict's case. But even if he was the coolest bachelor this side of the southern hemisphere, she needed a date with him like she needed a hole in the head. The men in her life had only caused her trouble. She didn't want to perpetuate the trend, so if Benedict Laverton tried to kiss her . . . she'd . . . she'd . . . Well, he'd just better not, that was all!

Rosy slammed off the water and grabbed a towel. She rubbed herself vigorously, muttering curses under her breath. All her previous good humor gurgled down the drain along with the soapy water. She wished Laverton was as easily disposed of. She mustn't foster any involvement with him. It wasn't personal. Men were simply not on her wish list, however gorgeous and tempting and . . .

Whoa! Hadn't she decided a long time ago that relationships were for mugs? She'd had a bad affair followed by a disastrous marriage and she wasn't game to get close to a man again. Life was much less complicated without a man. She must remember that.

She was in control of her life, such as it was, and she wasn't going to forfeit that for anyone, ever, and especially not Benedict Laverton.

* * *

He'd used too much of his mother's gel to hold down his cowlick, but his face was scrupulously clean and so was his shirt. The pockets of his trousers didn't bear scrutiny, but the pants themselves were almost crease-free.

Benedict eyed the diminutive Josh with interest as the boy held open the front door for him. 'You're looking smart,' Benedict acknowledged, though he wondered how long the gel would anchor down those wayward curls.

'Yeah, we're going out.' Two dimples appeared among the freckles.

'That so? Somewhere nice, I hope?' He followed Josh into the cozily cluttered living room where the demon dog that had inflicted so much pain summoned up a lazy tail wag in greeting. A large orange cat was curled on top of the television and blinked inscrutably. A piebald rat ran frantically in its exercise wheel and totally ignored him.

'The Laughing Duck,' said Josh.

'You got a hot date?' Benedict laughed before the penny dropped with an almighty clang. 'You're coming with us?'

Hold on a darn minute! Tonight's

dinner was meant to be an intimate meal for two, with a great deal of emphasis on the intimate bit.

'Mummy couldn't find a babysitter.'

How hard did Mummy try, that's what Benedict wanted to know? If she thought she could brazenly use her sons as half-pint chaperones . . .

'You don't mind, do you?' Matthew hesitantly asked from the safety of the doorway. Benedict was strongly tempted to tell him that he did flipping well mind. But the troubled, uncertain expression in the young lad's brown eyes, eyes so much like Rosy's, stopped him in his tracks. How could he trample over the lad's fragile feelings just because he felt frustrated and out-maneuvered? Benedict could empathize with Matthew. He remembered the feelings of isolation so well. It seemed his whole childhood had been one of aloneness, of being on the outside of other people's happiness.

Okay, so he wanted Rosy all to himself, but . . .

'Of course I don't mind. The more

the merrier.' He attempted to inject some heartiness into his voice.

'I told Mummy you wouldn't like it. That you might want to kiss her again.'

Yup, the boy was spot on. Smart lad. He'd go far. 'And what did Mummy say?'

'Mummy said you were a perfect gentleman and you were only carrying out your duty as per Deirdre Bott's orders. And everyone in Coolumbarup knows one has to jump when Deirdre says so!' said Rosy with robust sweetness, shooing Matthew into the room and brandishing a bottle of cheap supermarket sherry under Benedict's nose. 'Good evening, Mr. Laverton. Can I tempt you to a glass before we go? It's only cooking sherry, I'm afraid, left over from Christmas.' Rosy set down two Vegemite glasses and raised laughing eyes to his. 'We're the last word in style here.'

Benedict's heart slammed against his ribs as he held her saucy gaze. She really was a darling. How could he have ever thought her dull and dowdy with her toffee brown hair glinting with bronze highlights and her soft brown eyes as velvet and sweet as dark chocolate studded with golden honeycomb? Mascara had darkened and lengthened her already long lashes, blusher emphasized her deceptively fragile cheekbones, and the barest hint of lipstick made him want to lean forward and touch those sassy, kissable lips with his.

Benedict had never felt less like being a gentleman.

If Rosy's boys hadn't been in the room, he would have thrown her backwards on to the sofa and flung himself on top so he could kiss her senseless and take them both spiraling off into another dimension as their hands and their mouths moved to excite and pleasure each other . . . Benedict hastily rammed his hands into his trouser pockets to hide his hardening body and fought to get his brain into gear. He may have to be a gentleman tonight, but no one said anything about tomorrow.

'A sherry would be great,' he said, his voice smoky with suppressed desire. Whisky was his poison, but if sherry were the only thing offered it would have to do.

He tried not to grimace as he swallowed the first mouthful. Did people really cook with this stuff? He took another tentative sip. It was no better. With hooded silver eyes, he regarded Rosy. She positively radiated disgustingly good health in spite of their earlier hard footy workout and the abysmal sherry. She didn't even flinch when she swallowed.

There was no doubt about it, Rosy Scott was one tough cookie.

Rosy resisted the urge to hurl the sherry down her throat in one swift shot. Usually she didn't drink, but tonight she'd already had one while getting ready. She'd needed the bolstering to soothe her nerves. And it had taken her a lot longer than normal to dress. What was it about Benedict Laverton that made her jittery and unsure of herself? For heavens sake, it didn't matter what she wore. She wasn't out to impress this city slicker.

Nevertheless, she'd actually ironed her jeans, which she hadn't done since dating in high school, and had put on and discarded half a dozen tops before opting for her favorite, an unimaginative black stretch jersey. What to do with her hair had caused another bout of worrying. In the end, she'd twisted it up in a knot and allowed a few tendrils to feather her face. She'd carefully put on her make-up, going for a more understated look, which had been fine until she couldn't decide which lipstick to wear. She'd tried on three colors, scrubbing each one off in turn so by the end of it she didn't need any because her lips were red and throbbing from her ministrations.

And now the crunch had come. Mind, it had been pure genius to drag her boys along too. Hah, let's see how Mr. Smooth Laverton dealt with that. She resisted pouring out another rot-gut sherry. There was only so much a body could take of the foul stuff without ending up in the hospital's casualty department.

'Would you like a top up?'

Rosy bit back a laugh as Benedict recoiled at the suggestion. He couldn't have moved faster if she'd offered him a poisonous snake.

'Um, no, that was great. Really. I think it's time we were going. All of us.'

Rosy smothered another giggle. So he'd seen through her ruse. Hopefully he'd take the hint and leave her alone.

The four of them walked to the Laughing Duck. Benedict was all for taking his car, but Rosy airily waved the idea aside. 'It's only a hop, skip, and a jump away. Nothing is too far away in Coolumbarup. And anyway, the walk will improve your appetite.'

Benedict seriously doubted it. The pain of walking would annihilate any desire for food. But the Scotts were already springing to their feet and rushing out the door. He rose with great caution, trying not to wince at the painful twang of his overstretched muscles that failed to respond to Radox or the hideous tasting sherry. He manfully attempted to arrange his facial expression into one of eagerness. He bombed.

'You okay, Mr. Laverton?' Josh inquired with innocent solicitousness. 'You've got a very funny look on your face.'

'I'm fine, Josh, just fine,' he managed to say, unclenching his jaw just enough to answer the boy.

'Don't worry about him, lovey. He's only suffering from good, honest exercise.' Rosy robustly clapped Benedict on the back. He heard her snicker.

'Huh. I don't know what you're going on about. There's nothing wrong with me.' He tried to affect cool dignity, but the action of standing tall and pulling back his shoulders hurt like hell. Those footy players may have been little, but they had certainly shown no fear of tackling hard. He was proof of that. His sinews, muscles and every-thing else were screaming blue murder. But he'd do his damnedest not to let Rosy know it. He didn't want to be teased all evening.

It took them less than ten minutes to reach the Laughing Duck. For such a small restaurant, Benedict noted there were a staggering amount of cars parked outside and live music burst from the open windows with enough bass to double the Richter scale.

'Good grief, it's packed.' Benedict stared aghast at the crowd.

'What do you expect? It is Saturday night.' Rosy pushed open the door and was heralded by a fanfare of catcalls. The band changed tune mid-beat and gave a rendition of 'Big Spender'. She grinned. Perhaps she could have left the boys at home after all. She had all the chaperones she needed right here.

'Rosy, darlin',' shouted a young man from one of the busy tables, 'you didn't have to dish out all that loot. You could've had me for free.'

'With me thrown in for good measure,' chipped in his mate.

'And me,' said another.

Rosy laughed delightedly. 'Now you tell me, guys. But then again, I had to go and buy me a real man!' She half turned towards Benedict and yanked him forward, ignoring his resistance. She briefly glanced at his scowling discomfort. Her smile widened. 'And here he is, boys, the bachelor belle of the ball!'

There was a chorus of groans and grumbles. 'But he's a city slicker, Rosy. Hell, he even smells of girlie scent,' remarked a man standing next to the door.

Actually, the smell had been tantalizing Rosy. She'd recognized it from somewhere. She leaned forward and took a big whiff. Her brow creased. She sniffed again and it cleared. Aah! 'It's only Radox, fellas. I had Bachelor Laverton out training with my boys today. Maybe he wanted to loosen up a bit for tonight.' She waggled her eyebrows outrageously and the men erupted with laughter.

'I feel like a prize idiot,' Benedict ground out, as a young waiter led them to their table.

'What do you expect? You're the town's celebrity bachelor out on his big night. You're bound to get flak. Surely you realized that? Or doesn't the grand Mr. Laverton deign to be teased by the masses?'

'I can stand a bit of ribbing along with the best of them, but all this has been a surprise. I didn't know I was going to be sold at auction until I stepped over the town hall threshold last night. That's why I was so eager for you to bid for me.' Benedict grumbled. He yearned for the sophistication and impersonal covering of the city. This suffocating small town coziness, where everyone knew everyone, was giving him heartburn!

'Loosen up, Laverton. Enjoy yourself,' Rosy said. 'Then tomorrow you can pack your bags and whiz back to the big smoke. Just don't forget to kick the dust from your shoes before you go.'

'I might want to stay,' he said nastily. 'Then what would you do?'

She grinned. 'It wouldn't concern me. I'd have paid my debt.'

'If you think this,' he waved his arm in an arc, 'is an intimate dinner for two, you've got rocks in your head. Hell, there're more people here than at a grand slam final.'

'It's intimate for this town.' She fluttered her lashes at him, a teasing light flashed in her syrupy brown eyes.

Benedict bared his teeth in a parody of a smile. He leaned forward and snagged her fingers that were fiddling with a fork, imprisoning them easily in his large, tanned hand. 'Okay, Rosy Scott, we shall have a meal here tonight, in front of all these people. But next weekend, I'm going to take you out for a proper intimate meal where there will be no locals breathing down our necks and watching our every move, no ear-splitting music assaulting us, and certainly no children cramping my style.'

'You have style, Laverton? I'm impressed.'

'You will be, Ms. Scott. Just wait for next Saturday.'

'Fighting words,' Rosy remarked with a coolness she was far from feeling. Her imagination was running riot, wondering what sort of style Laverton was cramping. Just the touch of his warm fingers on hers sent bizarrely erotic messages to her brain. It must be the cooking sherry short-circuiting her usual savvy. She tried to retrieve her hand, but his fingers tightened and held her in place effortlessly.

She raised her eyebrows. 'But I don't want to go. This is our first and only date.'

'Really? I'll have to cancel my check then.'

'That's playing dirty.'

'So?'

'You wouldn't dare.'

'Never dare me, Rosy. I love a challenge.'

'If you cancel that check, the charity will be drastically down on its funds, we won't be able to buy the extra equipment needed for the hospital, and everyone will be bitterly disappointed. Then to cap it all, Deirdre Bott will kill me and my blood will be on your hands.'

'Humor me, then. All I'm asking for is one night.'

'Join the queue, mate. All the single men around here want a night with Rosy,' a lanky youth butted in, smirking at Benedict. 'You ready to order now?'

Rosy successfully freed her hand. She grinned slightly self-consciously at the lad. 'Exaggerating again, Paul,' she said.

'It's true,' said Paul. 'And I'm first in line. So, what are you going to have?'

'We haven't seen the menu yet,' said Benedict.

'We don't need to. We know it off by heart,' said Rosy. 'And really there's not that much to choose from. The boys and I will have steak, chips, and salad, thanks Paul.'

'Right, Rosy. And you, sir?'

Benedict realized he wasn't going to be given the opportunity to see a menu. He shrugged and regretted it as his shoulder and neck muscles protested. Through gritted teeth, he ordered a steak too.

'Are you very sore?'

Benedict gave Rosy a glacial glare. For a cozy package, she certainly had a caustic vein running through her. 'As if you care. But no, I am not sore.'

'Liar. You winced.'

'It was a twinge. I'm a touch stiff. Nothing a good back rub wouldn't put right.' His dark brows rose a fraction, in a mute question.

Rosy ignored his silent request. 'You'll have to wait until you get back to the city. We don't stretch to such services in the country.'

'But, Mummy,' Josh piped up. 'You rub people better at the hospital.'

Rosy gently cuffed her son's head,

causing his precariously anchored cow-lick to flick skyward. 'That's different.'

'Why? The people in hospital are sore too,' said Josh with deadly logic.

'Yes, Mummy. Why's it different?' Benedict asked with mock innocence, a smile tugging at the corner of his mouth.

'They need it. You don't.' Rosy's eyes danced.

'I might just check myself in as a private patient. Then you'd have to exercise a little succor to the lame.'

Rosy didn't trust the wicked glint in his rain-washed gray eyes. Or the humorous twitch of his lips. The thought of giving him a massage sent a disturbing warmness through parts of her that had been on ice since Steve had left. Hmph, Mr. Benedict Laverton was bad news for her serenity. The quicker he upped stakes and returned to the city, the better.

'Deirdre Bott is the nursing director. She's in charge of the private patients. She'd be doing the honors.' Rosy gave a throaty chuckle as Benedict's face froze in horror and he gave an involuntary shiver.

'I think I'll pass on that experience. She looks as though she did her apprenticeship with the Russian weight-lifters.' His eyes shimmered silver. 'You don't do private patients at home, do you?'

Rosy hesitated. She could lie, but the boys would immediately set the record straight and Laverton might reckon he had her on the run. Of course, he hadn't! But she didn't want him getting the wrong idea. 'Only friends,' she said.

'Can I be your friend?'

She ignored his wheedling tone. 'No.'

'Why ever not?'

Why? Because she didn't trust him one iota. He was too sure of himself. Too rich. Too smooth. And he was too damn scrumptious!

'I have enough friends.'

'One can never have too many. I'll be a good friend — an asset.' It sounded as though he was pitching a business deal.

Rosy wasn't swayed. He sighed and continued, 'I have loads of endearing qualities you'll learn to love.'

'Name one.'

Benedict cast around to think of one Rosy would approve of.

'See. You can't.'

'I can! I'm quiet, tidy, and housetrained.'

'So is our dog.'

Benedict wasn't sure if that was a compliment or not. He decided to press on. 'I'm organized and conscientious.' He glanced at her face. Her head was angled to one side and she was holding up her fingers as he listed his talents. He gave a slow, lazy smile. 'And I'm excellent with figures.'

Rosy snorted. 'Yeah! That's what I'm afraid of! Ah, good, here comes our meal.' She was relieved to change the subject. Benedict and figures didn't bear thinking about

Benedict grinned and settled himself back comfortably in his seat. Rosy Scott wasn't immune to him. He would keep chipping away at her reserve. He had failed to tell her he could also add patience and tenacity to his list.

A plate, stacked high with French fries, was placed before him. He presumed there was a steak buried somewhere beneath the chip mountain. A similar mound was put in front of Rosy, smaller hills for the boys.

'Want anything else, Rosy?' Paul asked.

'A carafe of water, please.'

'How about some wine?' Benedict asked.

'No, water is fine by me.'

'Live dangerously, girl.' Benedict ignored her nervous cough, shaking head, and waggling eyebrows. 'Do you have a wine list, Paul?'

'No need, sir. Red or white?'

'Red or white? That's it?'

'House red or house white,' Rosy interrupted with a giggle.

'Red, then, I think.' He looked doubtfully at Rosy as the young waiter disappeared. 'Did I make the right choice?'

'No, Laverton. I did.' She giggled some more.

'The wine's that bad?'

'Worse. But it makes a great drain cleaner.'

'Great. It looks as if my system is in for a treat.'

The food was reasonable, the wine unpalatable, and the ambience non-existent. But Rosy's casual banter with other diners, her gentle camaraderie with her children, and her downright teasing of him were something else.

Benedict couldn't remember when he'd enjoyed a meal more.

6

The carousers were well into their sixtieth verse of 'The Quartermaster's Store' as the Scott boys licked clean their chocolate sundae spoons.

'Hey, leave some of the silver plate on, boys,' Rosy teased, ruffling Josh's hair.

'Let's get out of here,' said Benedict.

'Not enjoying yourself, Laverton? I did suggest we skip dinner.'

'The dinner was fine.' Surprisingly so. 'But the rest of it is giving me indigestion.' He jerked his head at the singers.

'They're just happy.'

'Crazy.'

'They like to sing.'

'Caterwaul.'

'So you don't want to hang around for coffee?'

'Not here.'

Rosy nibbled her bottom lip. Nowhere else to go in Coolumbarup on an evening, except her place. She supposed they would have to all return there anyway, as Benedict had left his car parked outside the house.

'My place, then.'

'You're on.' Rosy noted the sudden lightening of his expression and she experienced an awful feeling that she would live to regret her offer. But what else could she have suggested?

They gathered their things and rose to leave as the singers crucified another verse. Benedict winced.

'Lighten up, Laverton. These blokes are just having a little harmless fun. They're not hurting anyone. And, heck, they sing pretty good.'

'If you're tone deaf.'

'Nah! They're so cute.'

Cute? Cute? These hulking farm lads with beer flushed faces and cracked voices? Rosy Scott wasn't only tone deaf, she had warped vision too. He threw her a skeptical glance. She grinned back.

'Very cute,' she murmured, goading him.

His eyes flew to her generous, smiling mouth. It was tantalizing. A shaft of heat rammed through him. It must be the rough house red giving him the sweats. Surely a smile wouldn't pack that much punch?

His eyes remained glued to her lush, curved lips. He swallowed. It was just a smile, for goodness sake. One smile. He'd been smiled at by many attractive women. But they hadn't seemed to cause the same impact that Rosy's sassy lips did. Hers caused an immediate physical punch in the solar plexus! Being around her was like being a hormone-driven teenager again. A single mum of two, in a plain, black top and jeans, grinning like a cheeky Cheshire cat, was causing a reaction that was wholly physical. So physical, he had to shove his hands into his trouser pockets. He scowled. All he wanted to do was kiss her. He knew what those rosy-red lips could do, cushioned succulently under his questing ones. He knew what she tasted like and he wanted to —

'You ready, Laverton? My boys are sleeping on their feet. I need to get them home. It's time for bed.'

Bed. With Rosy. If her kissing was dynamite, what would her love making be like?

'Laverton?'

He snapped to attention. 'Yeah, yeah, I'm coming.' He thrust his imaginings on ice. Now was not the time.

★   ★   ★

Benedict padded around the daffodil-yellow kitchen while Rosy put the boys to bed. He could hear soft murmurs and husky, warm laughter. It was all very homey and domestic. So what the hell was he doing here? He had an unwritten rule to steer clear of women with children. He wasn't cut out for cozy family life. He'd never experienced it himself and found the whole thing rather daunting. Like open-heart surgery or learning the Bossanova. Anyway, he liked his own company and had no desire to get caught up in a relationship. He wasn't a hermit by any stretch. He had plenty of friends. If he wanted the company of an attractive woman, he organized it on his own terms. But he wasn't interested in long-term commitment. And he really, really balked at the idea of getting involved with a readymade family.

So again, what the hell was he doing here?

He hunched his shoulders, stuffed his hands in his pockets, and stared through the window into the ink-black night. He should make his excuses and go, while there was still time. He was crazy to think Rosy Scott's kisses were better than anyone else's. It was just the unusual circumstances that made them seem special. It wasn't every day he kissed a strange woman in front of a packed audience because she, no correction, he had paid ten thousand dollars for the pleasure. It must have been the adrenaline rush that had given her kisses a magical edge.

He hunched lower. Who was he kidding? He hated to admit it, but last night's kiss had him hooked. And he wanted more.

No! Damn it. He didn't. He would leave. Rosy Scott was not the sort of woman to mess with. She was a lovely, decent woman with responsibilities. He had no place here. He would leave directly.

★　★　★

Rosy silently stood in the doorway and studied Benedict Laverton. She had prolonged the boys' bedtime rituals long enough. She couldn't procrastinate any more without it seeming suspicious. She had to face him on her own. It had been a long time since she'd had a man in her home at night. She was nervous. Mind, Laverton didn't look particularly relaxed either. She could read body language easily and his was screaming. Laverton had the troubled air of a stressed man. Why? She'd thought the whole point of tonight was for him to get her alone. Hadn't he hinted as much?

Perhaps he'd tired of her company and couldn't wait to leave? Disappointment twanged, which was ridiculous. She hadn't wanted to go out to dinner with him in the first place. She didn't want him hanging around. She gave herself a mental kick. Laverton had to go.

'So, you want a coffee or to quit while you're ahead?'

Benedict swung around as Rosy propelled herself into the kitchen, a bundle of nervous energy, fussing with the kettle, clattering with the cups and saucers.

'Coffee, thanks. I'm no quitter.' Now why did he say that? Hadn't he just decided to leave?

'I only have instant. Is that okay?'

He hated instant. 'Instant's great.' He watched her in brooding silence, cursing himself for his obsession to kiss her.

'White or black?'

'Black.'

'With or without sugar?'

'Without.'

'Biscuits or . . . '

'Damn the biscuits!' Benedict swiftly strode over to the pantry where Rosy hovered and slammed the cupboard door shut. He placed a hand either side of her, imprisoning her without a touch.

'Okay, I'll take that as a no for biscuits.' She spoke lightly, which belied the fierce explosion of excitement in her belly. Was he was going to kiss her? Could she bear it if he did?

Could she if he didn't?

She tried to keep her eyes bland and calm, pretending his proximity had no affect on her. But the sudden golden sheen of her eyes and the rash of goosebumps over her skin betrayed her. Her tension transmitted to Benedict. His own tenseness dropped away as he misread the signs.

'I'm not going to hurt you, Rosy.'

'I didn't think you would, Laverton.' She placed a hand on his thudding chest and shoved rock.

'But I do want to kiss you.' His words hummed on the air. Rosy swallowed nervously.

'Why? Because of the money? Because you want revenge?'

'The money? Revenge? Hell, no! I want to discover if our first kiss was a fluke.'

'A fluke?'

'Yeah.'

'It was. It was. Believe me.' Rosy struggled for breath as her oxygen count was reduced to zilch. He mustn't kiss her again. Just in case it wasn't a fluke.

'I don't believe you.'

'But you must. That kiss was undertaken in highly charged conditions. Emotions were running riot. You'd been drinking. I'd just spent a lot of your money . . . '

'Humor me.'

'I don't think so.'

'Please.'

'No.' It was barely more than a whisper. She couldn't. What if it hadn't been a one off? What if every time he kissed her she had instant meltdown?

'Please, Rosy.' His silver gray eyes were hypnotic. She shivered as his head lowered towards her.

'No.'

'Trust me. Just a kiss.'

Trust him? Not in a zillion years. He was dangerous. His kiss carried a punch that could deck a heavyweight. And she was no heavyweight, especially when it came to relationships. Skinny bantam-weight was more like it and one with the handicap of a soft heart.

His lips, warm and pliable, touched her determinedly rigid ones. He moved with smooth, practiced ease, gentle and sure. But her lips remained clamped together.

She would not respond.

She would not respond.

She would not respond. The mantra jack-hammered in her brain.

'You're right.' Benedict abruptly broke contact. 'It was a fluke.'

Rosy sighed. Her mouth relaxed into

a tilted curve of happy relief. Thank goodness he thought so. It'd been a close call. For a split second she felt safe, but it was of short duration. As she raised her puppy-brown eyes to his gray ones, she realized they were brimming with laughter and then Benedict swooped in for the kill and captured her lips once more. This time, he meant business. And this time her lips were soft, vulnerably parted, and ripe for tasting.

He didn't spare her. Though Rosy struggled to erect her defenses, she was powerless against his urgent, questing mouth as he sought to appease his obsession to kiss her. Lips, tongue, teeth all came into clever play. Fireworks exploded behind Rosy's eyes as heat roared through her body, flaming her blood, searing her skin, and destroying her control. She moaned against Benedict's mouth, in protest or acquiescence, she didn't know which, and it encouraged him to deepen the kiss further until Ferris wheels of fire burned in her belly.

But with all the heat, her hand remained frozen against Benedict's chest. The other was clamped to the pantry door handle, anchoring her so she wouldn't fling herself against his lean, hard body and enjoy more than just his mouth. All her concentration was on that mouth. He didn't attempt to touch her with his hands. They remained firmly on either side of her. It increased the tension a hundredfold. What if he decided to fold her into his arms? What if he stroked her skin? What if . . . ?

Benedict dragged himself away and held her eyes with his for one long, steady moment. 'No fluke,' he whispered a millimeter away from her tingling lips. She was sure she could detect bewilderment in his tone. And something else she couldn't quite define.

Was he going to kiss her again? Could she handle it without embarrassing them both with her spontaneous combustion?

'Rosy?'

'Mmm?' Even that minimal response took a huge effort.

'What are we going to do about it?'

'What?' Rosy struggled to focus on what he was saying rather than wondering if his lips were going to work their magic again.

'The lack of fluke.'

Rosy tried not to inhale his musky male scent. It was an alarming aphrodisiac she could well do without. It clouded her reason and stole her sanity. And he still hadn't touched her with his hands. Would she survive if he did? After all her good resolutions to keep men out of her life, about not getting involved, everything would be lost if he did. She was sure of it. His kisses were TNT packed. What would the rest of him be like?

No, she mustn't even consider it. She must be strong. There were the boys to consider, both in the long and short term. What if they came into the kitchen now? How would she explain it?

What effect would it have on them? She was being totally irresponsible. But, goodness, it was so wonderful after all this time, to be held and kissed and . . .

No! She mustn't go there!

'Rosy?' Benedict nibbled at the side of her slightly parted mouth and she jerked her head to one side to avoid him. 'Rosy?' His tone was insistent, demanding an answer.

'It'll go away.' Her own voice was strained. Not surprising. She felt as if she'd done a three-hour workout with weights.

'Will it?'

Rosy attempted a nonchalant shrug, but her shoulders were frozen with tension overload. 'Probably. If you keep away.' Her voice cracked. His steamy, sexy kissing had paralyzed her vocal cords.

'What if I don't want to?'

'You have to.'

'No, I don't. Not unless you come up with an extremely good reason. I think we have something very special here.'

'It's called lust. Don't put fancy tags on it, Laverton. It's simple lust.'

'There's nothing simple about it.'

'There is. You're not thinking with your head. You're concentrating on — other things.' Rosy broke off and rolled her eyes expressively.

'I'm no sex-starved teenager,' Benedict chuckled. Rosy could feel the thundering vibration through her hand glued to his chest. She snatched her hand away and curled the fingers tight into her palm so the nails dug into the soft flesh. She used the pain to keep herself centered on reality and not on the heated desire rippling dangerously through her body.

'I'm more than capable of controlling my baser instincts. My mind is in control,' he said. 'Though I'm perfectly aware of my body's desires.' He smiled slowly, wickedly and Rosy felt her cheeks burn.

'We're two consenting adults who appear to have a fantastic sexual chemistry. I would love to explore that

sexual chemistry. Enjoy it. Flow with it.'
His eyes gleamed with a silver heat that
made Rosy tremble. 'Wouldn't you like
to as well, Rosy? Don't you want to
unleash the passion between us and see
where it leads?'

'I know where it will lead, Laverton.
To the bedroom.' Rosy tried to block
the vision of tangled limbs and rumpled
sheets. 'You forget, I was married. I've
been there and done that. And it's left
me with no desire to start again.'

Benedict stilled. 'I wasn't talking
marriage.'

'I'm well aware of that.' Rosy hoped
she sounded sophisticated and worldly.
She didn't want a commitment from
him, so why was she feeling so miffed?
'I wasn't talking marriage, either. I was
referring to a relationship between a
man and a woman. It's no great shakes.
I wouldn't recommend it.'

'One bad relationship doesn't mean
that subsequent ones will also be bad.'

'True. But all my relationships have
been lousy and I'm not willing to stick

my neck out again. You can call me a wimp, but there it is.'

'I wouldn't dare call you a wimp,' Benedict bit out a laugh. 'You're one feisty lady. I've seen you in action as Super Coach! But I do think you're wrong to put yourself on ice and not exercise your passionate nature.'

Rosy shivered at the vision of herself on ice and being passionate. God, what was Benedict Laverton doing to her? She'd never indulged in erotic imagery until he came along twenty-four hours ago and gate-crashed her life. Until then, she'd been in perfect control of her body and her mind. Now, both were in heated chaos.

Benedict noted the golden shimmer of her eyes and the convulsive working of her pale, delicate neck. What was she thinking? He wished he knew. She was a bundle of contradictions. Frigid, dowdy bird one moment and feisty, sensual witch the next.

'In fact,' Benedict's voice dropped to a deep rumble that made her nerve endings shake like aspen leaves. 'In fact, princess, I think it's time for a little gentle exercise to limber you up and get you back in the swing. We don't want your muscles stiff and cramped when the game commences. A little stretch here . . . ' He caught her hands in one of his and pulled her arms high above her head. He easily held her captive against the pantry door and leaned closer, his body still not touching hers. 'And a little massage there . . . ' With his free hand, he made sweeping strokes down the side of her body, his fingers skimmed tantalizingly past her breasts, down over her ribcage and slim waist, to where her hips flared, and then back again. 'And the workout begins . . . '

Rosy's eyes widened into huge orbs at the swift, sure strokes. She felt trapped, helpless . . . aroused! Even the knowledge that her sons slept a few feet away in another room wasn't enough to dampen the fire caused by this sinfully attractive man.

'Laverton . . . '

'The name's Benedict . . . '

'Laverton!'

'Benedict.' His mouth was a hairs-breadth from hers. 'Say it,' he commanded with throaty menace. 'Say it, Rosy, or I'll . . . '

Rosy suddenly had an overwhelming urge to tease him. It seemed the safer bet. 'Or you'll what . . . Laverton?' Her eyes danced saucily, her mouth curved in a brazen, challenging smile. She'd always been a sucker for a challenge.

'Or, so help me, I'll kiss you senseless and take you here and now. Against the door, on the floor, wherever, until you plead for mercy.' His hands tightened warningly around hers, his eyes molten gray and churning.

Rosy forgot to breathe. The picture he wove robbed her of the power. His hand spanning her waist sent a soaring heat into her belly. His breath caressed her skin. His lips were so close and yet not closing the final space to meld with hers.

'I'd better call you . . . Benedict,

then,' she whispered. There was a heart's beat pause.

'Shame. I was looking forward to carrying out my threat.'

Rosy giggled, suddenly feeling braver. 'Poor lamb.'

'But it won't stop me from kissing you.' He closed the final space at last and claimed her mouth. She tasted so sweet, he wanted and demanded more. Rosy shuddered, moaned, and flowered under his roving lips and tongue. The hand on her waist began to inch upwards until it cupped one firm breast. Rosy gasped. Benedict's fingers teased the nipple so it hardened and pouted for more. He responded to the invitation and the delicious friction shot arrows through Rosy's bloodstream.

It was exquisite torture. Rosy wanted it to go on and on, but she knew it would be disaster if she did. She struggled to get her hands free so she could push him away. She didn't want to melt with desire, but it would be inevitable if Benedict didn't stop. Now!

Rosy cursed her weakness as Benedict's body leaned against her to frustrate her struggles. His body was hard and aroused. He wanted her and was ready for her. The knowledge was heady. It fuelled the desire rampaging through her body. She gave up the struggle with a sudden, carefree abandon and let the torrents of feeling wash through her. She forgot her vow of celibacy. She forgot about the boys. She forgot about all the sensible reasons why she shouldn't be doing this and surrendered herself to his lashing, licking tongue and pleasure giving fingers.

Benedict was aware of the exact moment she joined him in their passionate dance. His pulses had been simmering almost to the boiling point until that moment. Now his pulses raged as Rosy melted against him, opening herself up to him, angling her mouth so he could delve deeper, and rubbing her body against him so he could feel her curves and valleys. His body leapt to dive into her soft, inviting warmth. He wanted her. Now.

He wrenched his mouth from hers, released her arms and, yanked her into a tight, breath-defying embrace. 'I don't want to stop,' he murmured raggedly into her tousled hair.

'Then don't.' Her husky wantonness made him smile.

'We have to. Before we do anything we'll later regret. I'll come back tomorrow to discuss it, after we've both had a time to think.'

Desire must have fogged her brain. 'Think? Discuss? What are you babbling about? We know what we want. As you said earlier, we're two consenting adults with great sexual chemistry between us. What's there to discuss, Laverton?'

'The name's Benedict. Or are you asking for trouble?'

'If it's the only way to get a response out of you.' She snuggled into him, willing him to kiss her. He inhaled her light, sweet fragrance and savored the feel of her soft, inviting body, but he didn't kiss her again. 'We don't have to discuss anything,' she said. She didn't want to think. She wanted to feel. She didn't want to talk. She wanted to make love.

Smack! The realization hit her midships. Make love with Laverton! A man she'd only just met after years of shying away from any sort of male relationships. She was crazy! She stiffened within his arms.

'We have to talk about us and this lack of fluke,' Benedict said softly, nuzzling her neck.

'Us?'

Whoa! There was no 'us'. She didn't want involvement with anyone. This was all a horrendous mistake. She pushed against Benedict to give herself breathing space. She couldn't think straight within his embrace.

Benedict itched to pull her back into his arms, but he thought better of it. Who knew where it would lead tonight if he did that? Probably to bed and no matter how much he wanted that, it was too soon. He wanted more from

Rosy Scott than a one night stand. If he moved too fast, he had the feeling she would erect barriers and shut him out. Tonight, they'd been driven by passion. In the morning, she would probably hate him if they let this passion run its natural course. She wasn't like the other women he knew. They were worldly and well versed in love affairs.

He could tell Rosy was already putting barricades in place. Her arms were wrapped tightly around her waist. Her eyes had lost their golden, slumberous sheen and were now dark, brooding, and hooded by her thickly lashed lids. Benedict yearned to reassure her that everything would be all right. He wanted to hold her. Kiss her.

But he didn't.

He turned and walked away.

It was one of the hardest things he'd ever done.

7

'Bacon and eggs, Benedict?' Martha asked, as her son staggered into the kitchen and slumped into a chair the following morning.

'Toast only, thanks.' He carefully rotated a shoulder and winced.

'You don't look too well, darling.'

'Understatement of the century. I think it's the combination of junior football training and the Laughing Duck's house red. My head feels like a malfunctioning cement mixer and the rest of my body defies any description except pain.'

'A hearty breakfast with all the trimmings will soon sort you out.' Martha waved a large frying pan in the air and banged its bottom with a wooden spoon. Benedict winced again.

'No!' he said with feeling. 'Toast is all I can manage. Really. Even that might be pushing it.'

'Oh, well.' Martha reluctantly returned the pan to its hook above the stove and popped a couple of chunky slices of homemade whole-meal bread into the toaster. She then asked, as casually as possible, 'So, how did it go last night? Did you have a good time?'

'Mmm.' Benedict rubbed his fingers against his temples.

'Rosy Scott is such a sweet girl.' Martha watched Benedict stretch his back muscles and grimace. 'And she does massages.'

'Yes, I know.'

'Oh, you do?' Her fine eyebrows arched in pleasant surprise. She placed honey and marmalade on the table in front of Benedict. 'Well, you certainly look as though you could do with one.'

Benedict grinned crookedly at his less-than-subtle mother. 'I would love Rosy Scott to oblige and smooth out all the kinks and knots in my back and neck, but unfortunately I don't think she feels the same way.'

'Oh, you have discussed it, then.'

'Yep, and she informed me in no uncertain terms that she only did friends.'

'But she does everyone in town. I wonder why she said that?' said Martha, her brow creasing.

'Hmm, I wondered that too.' Benedict had his own theory, but he wasn't about to share it with his mother. He reckoned Ms. Scott didn't trust herself with him. The thought was tantalizing. He'd never been one to indulge in overt sexual fantasies, but the thought of Rosy in the role of masseuse and with all that oil . . .

'They do say she has a magic touch,' said Martha, adding the butter and toast to the table.

'Oh, she does,' murmured Benedict with feeling.

'I haven't been to her myself. I haven't needed to. But I do think you'd benefit, darling.'

No argument there. Benedict was sure he would and that the experience would be fantastic.

'And I do believe she has a clinic on Mondays. If you could stay on a bit longer, I could book you in?'

Brilliant! Benedict grinned at his mother. Once in a while, she came up with an ace suggestion. He did a rapid mental check on his work schedule. With a bit of juggling, he could steal a day from the office. He was owed plenty of time off and what was the point of being the boss if you couldn't go AWOL once in a while?

'I might just take you up on that. But perhaps you should book me in under your name, just in case there's a problem.'

* * *

'Honey, you are the talk of the town.' Janice, Rosy's neighbor and old school friend, spooned instant coffee into a couple of sky-blue pottery mugs and poured on the boiling water. 'Wish I'd been there to see it.'

'Hmph!' Rosy rolled her eyes, glad

Janice hadn't been anywhere near the ball. She loved her friend dearly, but Janice didn't have one sensitive, subtle bone in her body. She would have milked the occasion for all it was worth. Rosy grabbed yet another T-shirt from the wash basket, shook it out, pulled it into shape, and folded it neatly.

'So tell me again, how did you snag that gorgeous man?'

'How do you know he's gorgeous? You've never seen him.'

'His reputation precedes him. Anyway, they were talking about him in the deli this morning. Several of the customers were at the auction. According to one lady, she was prepared to re-mortgage her house to bid for the star turn. Of course, that was until she realized how dead-set you were about buying him for yourself. Ten thousand dollars! That was serious money, Rosy.'

'I've already explained, Janice, it wasn't my money.' Rosy flipped a maroon sweat-shirt out of the basket and repeated her shaking, pulling, and folding routine.

139

'And it was his idea.'

'I know, honey, but how lucky can you get, Benedict Laverton chose you from all the other women at the ball. You must've really appealed to him. What did you end up wearing? The last time I spoke to you, you were going to wear that dreadful brown thing.'

'I did wear that dreadful brown thing,' said Rosy, dryly. 'I had to. Josh tipped juice over the other one minutes before I was due to leave.'

Janice's mouth dropped open. 'And he still asked you? Wow. Just goes to show, beauty is definitely in the eye of the beholder.'

'Thanks a lot!'

'Not that you aren't attractive, my sweet. But you don't exactly advertise your femininity. I mean, look at you now. Your jeans saw better days at least a century ago and your T-shirt, I wouldn't even bother to put in my rag bag.'

'Don't be rude. I love these jeans. They're comfy. And this is my favorite T-shirt.'

'Honey, if your friends can't be honest with you . . . '

'Okay, okay, so I need some new clothes, but the kids come first. They both need clothes and shoes. And we really should buy shirts for the footy team.'

It was Janice's turn to roll her eyes. 'Let someone else worry about that. Don't be so obsessive about the team. Try for a sponsorship or something.'

'We need to get better before we can do that. We haven't quite mastered the game yet.' She sighed. 'Though not through lack of trying.'

'Anyhow,' said Janice, rapidly losing what little interest she had in the football team, 'it's you we've got to concentrate on. It's about time you smartened yourself up and tried to attract a man.'

'I don't want to attract a man.' Rosy held up two socks to see if they matched. They didn't. She rifled unsuccessfully through the basket. It seemed to be an unwritten house rule that the other socks would be missing.

She was a bit like an odd sock herself. She didn't expect to find a mate. Or want to, come to that. Though she had to confess, Benedict Laverton had tempted her to change her mind on that score. If she'd realized how dangerous he was, she would have repelled him at their first encounter. But she'd been too slow. Too out of practice in the mating game.

Ahh, but wasn't that what Laverton had said? And wasn't he planning to limber her up and resume the game? Her mouth went dry just thinking about it.

'Course you do,' Janice maintained, dunking a ginger biscuit into her coffee and popping it into her mouth. She chewed for a few seconds and swallowed. 'Every woman wants to feel attractive. And you're more than half-way there with Benedict Laverton.'

'How do you figure, Einstein?'

'Well, honey, the word is that your kiss on center stage just about steam cleaned the hall. And you told me the reason you bid was so Mr. Laverton didn't have to suffer the post-ball dinner, but he took you just the same. I reckon the man fancies you.'

'Hah!'

'And, as he's as rich as Croesus, according to my reliable sources. You don't want to thumb your nose at that. Imagine, no more worrying about the bills — heaven itself. No more macaroni and cheese for tea. Nice new clothes for you and the children. New footy gear, even. Now surely that's worth thinking about?'

'You're getting way ahead of yourself, Jan. We just ate dinner together. That does not constitute a gold ring and commitment. And, believe it or not, there's a limit to what I would do for the football team.'

'So there wasn't even a tiny spark of interest?'

Spark? Raging inferno! 'This is boring. Let's change the subject.'

'Ah, so there was. Ooo, Rosy! About

time too. It's been an age since you dated. You haven't been out with anyone since Steve left.'

'And I'm not going to start now!' Rosy said in exasperation. 'I have no intention of getting caught up with a man.'

'I know Steve hurt you, but it's time to move on.'

'It's not just Steve. There was Rick as well.'

'Rick? That was in the dark ages. You hadn't long left high school, so it doesn't count.'

'Jan, my luck with the opposite sex has been abysmal. I don't have a talent for picking honest, trustworthy, or reliable men. Rick convinced me he loved me, talked me out of my knickers, and then ran off with my best friend. Then Steve cheated on me repeatedly and ran off with my second best friend. I suppose I should be grateful he bothered to marry me first!

'So, my sweet, I shall tell you for free that I'm not going for strike three, however tempting the talent might be.'

'Not all men are like those two rats,' said Janice. 'You were just very unlucky.'

'Or stupid. Anyway, I have the boys to think about now. They're the only men I want in my life.'

'You'll end up a dried up, sex-starved old maid.'

'Infinitely preferable to being a dried up, broken-hearted one.'

'Better to have loved and lost and all that,' countered Janice, waggling her eyebrows.

'I'm not so sure about that. Anyway, I've done my loving and losing routine twice over and I don't feel as though I've gained much from the experience. It's only left me distrustful of men.'

'It wasn't true love. You simply haven't met your soul mate yet.'

'You're an incurable romantic, Jan.'

'And you're not? Who gives her sons handmade Valentine cards every year? And who cries through all the old movies?'

'Everyone cries through the old movies. That's why they were made.'

'I don't. You're just an old softie.'

Rosy was saved from answering by a rap on the back door. 'It's open,' she hollered and clamped shut her mouth quick-smart when Benedict poked his head around the door.

'Hi!' he said and his warm, honeyed voice sent Rosy's cells jitterbugging. 'May I come in?'

Rosy nodded, unable to speak. It was as if a small pilot light, deep in her belly suddenly flared into full, roaring life. She could feel the flames licking through her body and hoped her skin wasn't scorched red, betraying her inner heat.

Had Benedict come to 'discuss' last night? Lord, how she wished there was nothing to discuss. She felt decidedly nervous having him here. It was easy to dismiss him from her life when he wasn't around. But in the flesh, he was a huge danger to her equilibrium.

He was looking good, even if there was a tiredness around his silver gray eyes which suggested he hadn't slept well. Well neither had she. She'd endured hours of sleeplessness, trying to quash those long buried feelings of desire that had shot to the surface at his first touch.

Now those feelings had been unchained, they weren't going to go easily back into the secret, locked room of her soul. She'd pummeled her pillow, drank a gallon of chamomile tea, and played all the meditation CDs she owned. In the end, it had been sheer exhaustion that had sent her into a deep, dead sleep just as the sky was lightening for the new day. A couple of hours later, the boys had been bouncing on her bed telling her it was breakfast time.

At least it was comforting to know she wasn't the only one suffering here.

Benedict was still holding his body stiffly. Obviously yesterday's footy work-out was still taking its toll. The knowledge helped her get perspective on things. He was just a man, a mere mortal. Nothing more. Nothing less. She was a fool to think otherwise.

'Meet my friend and neighbor, Janice Stone,' Rosy said, her voice husky in spite of her inner pep-talk. She coughed, to get her vocal cords to work properly. She didn't want Benedict getting the idea he had an effect on her. 'Jan, this is Benedict Laverton, the star of the Bachelor Ball.'

'Hello, Janice. Pleased to meet you.'

'And I you. I've heard so much about you.'

'You have?'

Rosy fielded Benedict's startled, wary glance. No doubt he was wondering just what she'd been saying to Jan. As if she'd let on to anyone what had gone on last night!

'Oh, not just from Rosy.' Jan grinned and Rosy inwardly groaned. Janice was making it sound as though she'd given him a blow-by-blow account, or was it a kiss-by-kiss?

'The whole town has been keeping me up to scratch,' Janice said and winked. 'Anyway, I'd best be off. I've lots to do.'

'Stay!' Rosy almost barked the command, her cells jitterbugged at the thought of being alone with Benedict. 'Have another coffee. You too, Laverton, I mean Benedict.' Too late, she realized her mistake. His silver eyes flashed and his mouth twisted quizzically. Last night's threat hovered between them. The jitterbugging increased and Rosy hurriedly went to make the coffee to hide her confusion.

'Don't let me cut short your visit,' said Benedict to Janice, as Joshua ran into the kitchen and said, 'Hi, Mr. Laverton. Have you come to play footy with us?'

'Well. Ah. I hadn't exactly planned to . . . '

'Aw, please!'

Benedict had no defense against the small freckle-faced boy with the big dimples and pleading eyes. 'Okay, I'll come and have a quick kick around, but in a while. I want to talk to your mum first.'

'Don't worry about me,' said Rosy

149

quickly. Perhaps too quickly? 'Go and have some fun while the kettle boils.'

She was glad of the brief reprieve, but it was obvious Benedict wasn't. His pained expression gave the impression that playing footy was akin to torture.

'Five minutes, kid. That's all I'm fit for today.'

'You betcha, Mr. Laverton.' Josh grabbed his hand and yanked him towards the backdoor.

'Excuse me,' said Benedict to the two women.

'Take your time!' said Rosy. He regarded her suspiciously before allowing Josh to pull him into the backyard.

'He's gorgeous!' said Janice as the fly screen door snapped shut behind him. 'How can you be so casual about him? I'd be swooning at his feet.'

Rosy was glad her friend hadn't picked up that she was swooning on the inside! Instead Rosy shrugged. 'I told you before, my track record is lousy. I don't want to put the boys and myself through the turmoil of another doomed affair.'

'Who said it would be doomed?'

'Me. I'm not a man-keeper, Jan. So there's no point even starting something with Laverton. Besides, I simply don't have dating skills anymore.'

'Practice.'

'What?'

'Practice. On Benedict. Might as well. You've got nothing to lose and a huge amount to gain if it works.'

Rosy threw back her head and laughed. 'You have got to be kidding me. He'll burn me up.'

'Ooo! He's that good? So what did go on last night?'

'Not enough,' said Benedict from the backdoor and almost gave Rosy a heart attack. 'But I'm working on it.' He grinned at her and she felt faint. A slight sheen of sweat had given a rich luster to his olive skin. His hair was rumpled from running. He looked sexy as sin.

The pilot light burst into full flame again, causing a swirling heat in her belly. She schooled her features into what she hoped was a disapproving frown at his comment and tried to ignore the heat.

'How's the coffee? Nearly ready?' said Benedict, apparently unaware of her inner chaos. 'Because I'm dying for a caffeine fix. Without it, I can't cope with the little fellas' tactics. Or the dog's.'

'It's not ready,' Rosy croaked. 'I'll call you when it is.'

As he disappeared again, Janice clasped her hands in front of her heart and sighed dramatically. 'I think I'm in love.'

'What about Lee?' Rosy caustically reminded her. 'You've got a perfectly lovely husband waiting for you at home.'

'I know. And he's a poppet, but that Benedict. He's something else! Are you sure you don't want a scorching affair with him?'

'No!' She thought of the previous night.

'Not particularly.' Being held in his arms.

'Not really.' Feeling his fingers on her skin.

'Well, maybe not for a while.' His lips seducing hers.

'At least not until the boys are older.'

Janice snorted. 'He won't wait around until Joshua is shaving!'

'Anyway, it won't happen. I'm not in his league.'

'He seems to want to put you there, though, if you ask me.'

The kettle began to shrilly whistle. Rosy snapped off the switch and leaned back against the counter, wrapping her arms protectively around her waist. 'I'm nothing more than a challenge for him. A bit of a novelty, that's all. He'll lose interest soon enough.'

'Don't be so sure,' said Janice.

'Yes, don't be so sure,' said Benedict, reappearing at the door like an irritating jack-in-a-box. He smiled at Rosy, his face suspiciously bland.

Just how much had he heard?

'I was just about to call you,' she said, feeling her cheeks redden.

'I pre-empted you. I was listening for the kettle's whistle.' He sat down at the table where Rosy's knickers were haphazardly stacked. He leaned his elbows on the table as his gaze dropped to the frayed, sensible cotton briefs. His eyes lifted to Rosy. She blushed deeper and whisked up the offending articles and tossing them back into the wash basket, before scooping up the other piles of clothes and placing them neatly on top, completely burying the knickers. Janice was right. She should invest in some new clothes, starting with some decent underwear!

Still feeling hot and bothered, she clicked Benedict's mug of coffee down in front of him.

'Well, I'd best be going,' said Janice. 'There's Sunday lunch to cook for the masses. Lee will be back with the kids any moment. Hope we'll see you around, Benedict.'

'You can bet on it.' Benedict smiled.

Rosy sat down for all of two seconds after Janice had left, but proximity to Benedict was giving her the twitches. She sprang to her feet and pulled out the ironing board from a cupboard. She set it up by the counter and then fetched the iron.

'What are you doing for lunch?' Benedict asked.

Rosy eyed him warily. 'The usual.' She tested the heat of the iron and then hefted it across Matthew's school shirt.

'Which is?'

'Something easy here at home.'

'So I won't be in the way if I stay?'

'Oh, well . . . '

'It's just I'm on my own. My mother has gone out for lunch with friends and I don't fancy eating alone.' He'd stretched the truth. His mother had invited him. But he'd declined, preferring to go his own way, especially when that way took him to Rosy Scott.

'Don't you have to return to the Big Smoke?'

'No rush. But, if it's too much trouble, I won't stay.' Benedict decided to play to her soft heart. Hadn't she proved she had one at the auction?

It worked a treat.

'No, of course not. It'll only be scrambled eggs on toast, mind, but you're welcome to join us.'

'Thanks. I'll look forward to it.' Benedict drained his coffee. 'Now, I'd best get this over and done with,' he said with a martyred air, nodding towards Rosy's backyard where the thump of a football could be heard along with the boys' raised voices and the dog's excited yipping.

After he'd left, Rosy rested her forearms heavily on the ironing board and bowed her head. This wasn't going to plan at all. As the steam iron hissed and popped, Rosy sighed. She tiptoed over to the window and peeked out. There was a lot of jostling going on, lots of barking, shouting, and laughter. Benedict was letting the boys and Henry trash him. He'd have to get into better shape if he kept coming around.

Whoa! Don't go down that road. This was probably just a once off. She couldn't imagine Benedict choosing to be tackled into the dirt by dogs and children on his weekends. He was too much the city slicker. Shouldn't his weekends be taken up with civilized golf on immaculate greens and meals at the most exclusive eateries Perth had to offer? Hers consisted of mountains of wash, ironing, cleaning, and preparing for the week ahead. And, of course, footy training. There was nothing remotely jet-set about Rosy's weekends.

Rosy resumed her ironing and tried to concentrate on the rhythmic sweeps of the iron over cotton to soothe her troubled mind. There was no point wasting energy and emotion to fathom Benedict Laverton and his motives for seeking her out. She would just have to wait and pray it had nothing to do with last night's kisses.

'Lunch time. Come and clean up!' she hollered from the back door half an hour later.

While they washed their hands, Rosy whisked up the eggs and cooked the toast, cutting the slices into squares. She spooned on the eggs and then placed the plates in front of the boys and Benedict. It was only as she put Benedict's meal down, she realized what she'd done.

'Oh, I'm sorry. I've cut up your toast.' She sucked in her lower lip. What a stupid thing to do. The man must think her a moron. She hadn't been thinking. Too preoccupied with the impact Benedict Laverton was having on her life.

'I don't mind. I haven't had my food cut up for me since I was six.'

Matthew dropped his eyes to his plate. 'Mum still cuts up mine, as if I was a baby,' he said.

'It's a force of habit, darling,' said Rosy, ruffling his hair.

He pulled away. 'But I should do it myself. I'm seven.'

Benedict wondered what was going on in the lad's head. There was obviously something troubling him. It wasn't the first time Matthew's comments and behavior had struck a long forgotten chord in Benedict. He decided to try and work out exactly what was upsetting the boy, but he knew he'd have to tread carefully. 'I didn't want to cut up my own food,' he said conversationally, 'but I had to. I was sent to boarding school.'

'At six?' Rosy was appalled. The boys stared at him bug-eyed, food momentarily forgotten.

'I was an only child,' he shrugged. 'My parents traveled around a lot with my father's work. It was the best thing for me.' Or so they thought, he silently added, remembering the deep sense of betrayal he'd suffered at being left behind.

Matthew and Josh acted as if he'd sprung a million heads. 'You didn't have your mummy reading you stories and kissing you night-night?' asked Josh, his fork mid-air, dripping egg.

'Nope. I had a ferocious matron as ugly and big as an ogre who used to march up and down the dormitories making sure we were all in bed and the lights were out.' He'd ached for his mother's touch, her warmth, her smell. Recalling that time, he was surprised he still felt the betrayal keenly.

'Could you have your teddy with you?' Josh persisted.

'Yes, but if you did, you didn't tell anyone. You hid him down the bottom of your bed and hoped no one would find him.'

'If they did?'

'You were teased terribly.'

'Did you have a teddy?' Josh said.

'Ah, that's classified information.' Benedict grinned.

'What does that mean?' asked Josh.

'It means Mr. Laverton isn't telling,' said Rosy, trying to keep the waver from her voice.

Benedict glanced at her and was surprised to detect a gleam of moisture in her expressive puppy-brown eyes, moisture she rapidly blinked away once she realized he was watching her. He gave her a gentle, quizzical smile. 'It's okay, sweetheart. It was a long time ago,' he said.

Rosy gave a sharp sniff. 'Hmph! It's nothing to me.'

Benedict reached across the table and touched the corner of her eye where the moisture had pooled.

Rosy jerked back and blinked again. 'I've got an eyelash caught, that's all!'

'Ah.' Benedict flicked the tear with his forefinger. An unusual warmth spread through him. Someone feeling sorry for him was a strange sensation. He'd stood alone all his life, being relied on by others, being called on to sort out their personal and business problems. He couldn't remember the last time someone had actually felt his pain. He rocked back in his seat and stared at Rosy, his eyes purposefully hooded so she couldn't read any of the emotions roaring through his soul.

But she wasn't looking at him anyway. She was fiddling about with the sugar bowl, mining the granules with the stainless steel spoon in an attempt to look cool and detached. She was an interesting, complex woman and one who caused him a whole gamut of feelings, desire, tenderness, and curiosity among them. He experienced a sharp thrill of anticipation. This affair was not going to be like the others. He looked forward to the challenge of seducing and enjoying the gorgeous Rosy Scott.

'Rosy?'

She jumped, sending a spray of sugar over the Formica topped table. 'Yes?'

'I think it's time we talked.'

'Not now?' He noted the flare of panic in her eyes, the tightening of her hold on the spoon so that her knuckles whitened.

'Why not? Because of the boys?'

'Yes, and I have a couple of massage clients this afternoon.'

'Oh. Tonight, then?'

'Can't. I've got training.'

'Footy?' Grief, she was keen. He didn't think he would survive another workout so soon after the last one.

'No. Running. I've entered the hospital's charity fun run.' A smile suddenly lit her face and banished the earlier wariness. In fact, she looked downright crafty in Benedict's opinion. 'You could join me if you like?' she said, obviously betting that he wouldn't want to.

'No.' said Benedict. He paused for a second, as the smug smile tugged at the corners of her kissable mouth and he tried not to grin too. He let her savor her short triumph. 'Not this time, but I'd like to have a go some other day when I can reschedule my work. I enjoy a brisk few miles when time allows.'

The swift panic that flooded her face almost made Benedict laugh out loud. She might run for charity, but Benedict knew he had Ms. Scott running for a very different reason.

Now all he had to do was get into training when he returned to the city so he could keep up with her when they did finally hit the road together. He was sure she wouldn't cut him any slack. And he wouldn't want her to. Just as he wouldn't cut her any either. They were equals.

This, he decided, was going to prove a very rewarding relationship. He hadn't been this interested in a woman in years.

8

'Is Martha here yet?' Rosy poked her head around the door of her spare room that doubled as her massage surgery and scanned the faces of those waiting to see her. 'No?' Her eyes alighted on Benedict. 'Oh. Hi.' She straightened in surprise and then pursed her lips. Hmm, what was he doing here? Come to hassle her? She wasn't sure if she felt pleased or not. It was flattering having a man like Benedict Laverton interested in her. But it was also rather disturbing. What exactly did he want from her?

'Okay, Chrissy,' she said to a birdlike woman sitting next to Benedict, 'you'd better come in next.'

She cast a puzzled frown in Benedict's direction and then a nasty thought struck her. Don't say he was the one with the appointment? A prickle of panic pierced her calm. Maybe the appointment hadn't been for Martha after all. She'd been duped into massaging Benedict! Lordy! And after categorically telling him she only did friends. Huh, she should have guessed he wouldn't give up so easily. Well, neither did she.

She smiled at Chrissy as the woman rose to her feet. 'Nice talking to you,' said the older woman to Benedict. 'Hope to see you around, Ben.'

Rosy bit back a snort and spun back into her massage room. Goodness, did every woman respond to Laverton's charm? Chrissy Barlow was simpering like a Jane Austen heroine and she was all of sixty-five with a bevy of grandchildren under her belt. Rosy shut her surgery door with a sharp snap. Benedict Laverton was too much.

★ ★ ★

Benedict and a younger man were the only ones left in the waiting room, but not for long. Joshua rushed in from the garden, a book clutched between his

166

grubby hands, and said, 'Mr. Laverton, hi! You gonna read to me?' He tugged at Benedict's arm. 'It's a 'citing book.'

'In that case, how could I resist?' Benedict smiled at him.

He was a bit taken aback when Josh unselfconsciously climbed into his lap, kneed him in the groin, and then made himself at home like a bony, leggy cat. Once comfortable, he handed the book to Benedict and stared at him expectantly. Benedict felt awkward. He'd never read to a child before. He wasn't quite sure what was expected of him. He cleared his throat and haltingly began to tell the story.

'Stop,' said Josh, fixing Benedict with a serious stare. 'You have to do the giant's voice big and deep.'

'Oh, right. Like this?'

'It's okay, but Mummy does it better.'

'I'm sure she does. Well, like this then?'

'Deeper, like you gotta cold. Mum goes all husky.'

Benedict was immediately transported back to Saturday night and Rosy's voice, passion-fuelled and sexy, huskily asking him to stay. Somehow he didn't think that was quite what Josh meant. He mentally shook his head at the memory. Now was not the time to listen to that sexy echo. He had a kiddies' book to read.

The other man went in for his massage and a while later, three books later by Benedict's reckoning, he came out with a big grin on his face. 'Thanks, Rosy, I feel so much better. Like a new man,' he said.

Benedict experienced an unexpected sharp stab of jealousy. Damn it, what was happening to him? He'd never been the jealous sort and all the bloke had done was get a massage.

A massage by Rosy — her small, capable hands running over his body!

Benedict all but gnashed his teeth. Hell, he wanted her hands on his body. The young buck looked much too darned pleased with himself. Benedict didn't trust that self-satisfied look. Not at all.

'Good,' Rosy was saying, 'but don't forget those exercises or you're wasting your time and money coming here. See you next week.'

The man nodded to Benedict as he went out. Rosy steeled herself to do battle with Benedict. 'So,' she said, hands on her hips, 'no Martha? What a surprise.'

Benedict smiled in what he hoped was a beguiling way. 'You don't mind, do you?'

'Yes, I do as a matter-of-fact.'

'Aw, Rosy, I asked her to book it because I thought you'd knock me back cold.'

'Yep, you're right there.'

'But I'm in pain.' He moved his arm and gave an exaggerated groan.

Rosy rolled her eyes. 'Poor baby.' But she didn't sound very sympathetic.

'Yeah, that's me. And it was all due to your footy training, Coach.'

'No-one asked you to play.'

'And your dog.'

'He wasn't invited to play either.'

'But he did, encouraged by your team. You have to take full responsibility and make amends.'

They stared at each other for a long, assessing moment. Benedict held his breath, hoping she would say yes. He could tell by her narrowed eyes and pursed lips that she was going through all the reasons why she should say no.

Josh piped up in the static silence, 'What about my story? Come on, Mr. Laverton, read it.' He jabbed his sharp little elbow into Benedict's ribs.

'Oof!' said Benedict.

'Josh!' said Rosy. 'Say sorry.'

'Sorry. Read it. Read it!' He jiggled about enthusiastically.

'Say please, Josh,' said Rosy.

'Please,' said Josh dutifully. Benedict raised inquiring brows to Rosy. She huffed then shrugged.

'Okay. Once you're done with the story, I'll give you a massage.'

Eureka! Benedict tried not to look smug, but he could feel his lips curve into a grin. Curb it, he told himself or she'll backtrack. He concentrated on the story for all he was worth, though afterwards he couldn't have said what it was about. All his focus was on Rosy and imagining her massaging him with those small hands and lots and lots of lovely oil. It was enough to make him blow a fuse.

Rosy went into the kitchen to prepare dinner, keeping half an ear cocked on Benedict's low, rumbly voice. It was melodic, pleasant, and nice. Too nice. She tried not to tune into it and concentrated fiercely on sprinkling some herbs and lemon pepper on lamb chops and put them in the oven. She scrubbed some small potatoes and put them in too.

She washed and dried her hands and then stood in the doorway, arms crossed, her shoulder leaning against the jamb, watching Josh cuddling up to a man who was, until a couple of days ago, a complete stranger. Benedict Laverton had bulldozed into her life and was blithely re-landscaping the safe boundaries she'd set for herself after Steve had left. It was galling how much impact he'd had on her. It worried her. His presence was too unsettling. It was time he went back to wherever he belonged and let them all get on in peace. But first, she had a massage to do.

As Benedict finished the story, she eased herself away from the doorjamb and said, 'Okay, Laverton, you fit?'

Fit wasn't a description he'd have used. He was as stiff as a piece of uncooked spaghetti. Even stiffer than Sunday, and that was saying something. Nevertheless, he got to his feet with an alacrity that surprised them both and followed Rosy into the massage room.

'Just how hurt are you?' she asked suspiciously, deciding there and then to use on him the most relaxing oils she had. It would hopefully render him comatose and therefore less dangerous. It was her secret weapon.

'Very.' He brushed past her and into the room, hoping she wouldn't see his guilty grin. He heard her sigh behind him, acknowledging defeat. His grin flashed out, but he hid it again immediately.

The room was light and airy with pearl pink walls and pale floral curtains. It was less of a statement than Rosy's yellow kitchen. It was designed to calm and relax rather than stimulate. And it was redolent with the aroma of oils — lavender, rose, sandalwood, and others he couldn't quite identify. He stood in the middle of the room and waited for Rosy to tell him what to do.

She didn't fail him. 'Strip,' she said matter-of-factly.

'Excuse me?'

'You heard, Laverton.'

He experienced a rush of blood and was momentarily light headed. 'Do you tell all your clients to shed their clothes?' he said incredulously. Another shaft of pure jealousy speared him in the gullet. Had that hulking farmer boy been naked here minutes before?

'What do you think?' Rosy took out some clean, navy towels from a closet and spread them on the massage table.

Benedict slowly undid a button. 'I'm not sure what to think.'

Rosy eyeballed him. 'Hurry up, Laverton. I don't have all day.'

'Yes, ma'am.' He dealt with the remaining buttons and hauled off his shirt to reveal gridiron shoulders and a taut stomach.

'Mmm, not bad for an office boy,' said Rosy.

Benedict's lips twitched upwards. 'I'm glad you approve.'

Rosy gave a derisive snort. 'This is work, Laverton. Don't get cocky.'

'So how far do you want me to go?'

'How far are you willing?'

Benedict hesitated. Suddenly he didn't think he could brazen it out. It was different when there were two of you stripping off, but just him, with Rosy watching. His nerve failed him!

Then he caught the flash of laughter in Rosy's eyes. She was teasing him! Hah, well two could play that game. He swiftly peeled off his black jeans, socks, and jocks.

There was a heart's beat pause.

Rosy gave him a rapid inspection. She couldn't help herself. Wow! He was a sight to behold. And some! She clamped down on a rush on tingles. This wouldn't do. She had to exercise huge control not to show how much he was affecting her.

Benedict levelly watched her, wondering what came next.

'Nice,' said Rosy.

'Cute,' she said as her eyes did a more thorough roam.

'Now put your jocks on.'

Benedict sucked in a quick breath, non-plussed by her turn around. Rosy grinned at him. He recovered quickly. 'Can't handle having me butt naked?' he said softly, his eyes glimmering hot silver.

'Sure I can handle you, Laverton. Just lie back and see.' She dropped her eyes and squeezed a dollop of oil onto her hand. She began to rub it vigorously, too vigorously in Benedict's opinion, between her palms.

'Professionally, maybe. But privately?' he said.

'We're only talking professional here. There'll be no private. Now are you just going to stand there and talk or put your jocks on and get on the table?'

'Why bother with the jocks?' Benedict challenged. 'I don't want any clothes hampering your massage.'

Rosy pinked beautifully. Benedict did his best not to smile. He'd out bluffed her.

'You have to put them on,' she said.

'Why?'

'Because.' She paused. 'Because if anyone comes in here and sees you naked, they'll begin to wonder what goes on here. I could lose my business. And I need my business, Laverton, to put food on the table for my boys.'

'Okay, seems a fair enough reason to me.' Benedict casually pulled back on his jocks and climbed on to the table. 'Back or front first?' he queried, humor glinting deep in his silver gray eyes.

No contest!

'Back.' Then he couldn't see her expression or her blushes or her curious, hungry eyes devouring his beautiful body!

Rosy hands slid over the wide expanse of his back. Benedict groaned as she found a knotted muscle and worried it with her strong, sure fingers. She worked in silence for a while. The only sound was her palms, oil slick, skating over his firm flesh and Benedict's groans and sighs of pain and pleasure.

'So,' she said after a while, 'did you take teddy to boarding school?' The idea of such a small boy being sent away had wrung her heart. She could never do that to her boys. Underneath her fingers, she felt Benedict tense. His muscles knotted.

'Did you?' she asked again, kneading his stiff shoulders.

'Why do you want to know?'

'Curiosity. Why don't you want to tell me?'

'It's not that I don't want to tell you, but it was a long time ago. It's not important.'

'The way your muscles have suddenly cramped, I'd say it is still an issue with you.'

He sighed. 'Don't you ever give up?'

'Nope.'

'Aren't you just supposed to rub me into a state of paradise? In silence?'

'Nope. I'm also father confessor to my clients. They like to unburden themselves to me. It helps the relaxation process.'

Benedict twisted around. 'Mother,' he said.

'Sorry?' She sucked in her bottom lip, staring into his shimmering gray eyes, wishing he hadn't turned to face her. She felt far too vulnerable having him semi-naked under her hands.

Of course, it would be even worse the other way round! She quickly deleted that naughty thought. This was not the time to fantasize.

'Mother confessor. There's nothing remotely masculine about you,' said Benedict.

'That's not what Janice thinks,' she

muttered, forcibly pushing Benedict back down on his front.

'What does she know?' Benedict said, his voice muffled by the towel.

Rosy grinned. 'Not a lot,' she said, suddenly cheerful. She scooped up another dollop of oil and ran her hand across his shoulders. 'So, about teddy?'

'Yes. I had a teddy.' He'd gone taut again under her fingers. The subject obviously bothered him. She kneaded briskly. 'He was golden and furry with a button nose. His name was Hercules.'

'And did he enjoy boarding school?'

'He never made it there.'

'Oh, but you said . . . '

'I lost him on the way there. Probably on the train.'

'Oh, Benedict, how terrible.' Rosy's hands stilled. She felt the pain of a little boy lost in the system without anything familiar to love. She considered how Matt and Josh would cope without their favorite toys snuggled in bed with them.

'I must have cried for a week,' Benedict said, his voice still muffled. 'I think I missed that bear more than my mother.'

'I'm sorry.'

'What for? It wasn't your fault and it was a long time ago. I survived. I'm a big boy now.'

Rosy sighed and began kneading again. 'So apart from that shaky start, did you enjoy boarding school?'

'No, I hated it. I vowed if I ever had children, I would never send them away to school.'

Again, Rosy stopped massaging. 'I suppose we should be grateful something positive came of your experience.' She resumed rubbing with a lot more force than before. 'I couldn't bear to send my boys away.'

'No, I shouldn't think you could. But then you're a lot different from my mother.'

'Martha's a lovely lady,' Rosy said simply.

'Yes, she is, but she's not the maternal sort. She was much more wrapped up in Dad than me. She adored him and he adored her. There wasn't much room for a scrawny kid. I cramped their style.'

'You're exaggerating.'

Benedict was silent. He remembered the holidays. He was either left at the school in charge of one of the bachelor masters, billeted with distant relatives because his parents were off abroad somewhere and unable, or he suspected unwilling to have him. He'd hated term times, but the holidays were worse. He had detested them with a passion.

'All mums love having their kids at home,' Rosy said. 'In fact, if I'm honest, I need them more than they need me. I'd be lost without them.'

'Where's their dad?' Benedict asked. The hands stopped. 'Rosy?' He twisted around to try and see her, but Rosy shoved his head back down.

'It's none of your business, Laverton.' Her brisk efficiency was back in place.

Benedict gave a muffled laugh into the towel. 'So it's okay for me to spill out my heart about my old teddy bear, but you're allowed to stay mute about your ex-husband. Where's the fairness in that?'

'There isn't any. You have a problem with that?' Rosy dug her fingers into a particularly tender spot.

Benedict yelped. 'No! Yes! Ouch! No! I surrender.'

'Good. Now shut up so I can give you a thorough going over.'

'Ms. Super Coach is back in harness.'

'Believe it!'

Benedict fell silent, his teeth gritted against the busy, probing fingers that instinctively found every sore spot he didn't know he had.

What was the big deal about Rosy's ex-hubby? What had she said the other night about relationships? That she didn't rate them highly? Hell, everyone had duff times, but it didn't mean every relationship had to be terrible. Her husband must have treated her extremely badly to make her so suspicious. Benedict vowed he'd find out exactly what had gone on and deal with it. If he didn't, their relationship would be unable to progress and, if one thing was certain, Benedict wanted to take things further with Rosy. The more time he spent with her, the more he wanted and he wouldn't be put off by the specter of an ex-husband.

Rosy watched her hands glide over the wide expanse of muscled flesh. The skin was tanned as if Benedict spent time outdoors, perhaps swimming. She could easily imagine him in the surf, water glistening on his torso, salty droplets in his hair. Her throat went dry. She determinedly swallowed. Keep your mind on the job, she admonished herself. Soon she would have to tell him to flip over so she could do his front.

But, no! She didn't think she could do it. Mentally she kicked herself. Come on, Rosy. You massage people all the time. You've seen stacks of bodies.

But not this one, her inner voice said. Not Benedict Laverton's.

Having him prone on her massage table was causing her severe problems, not the least of them breathing. No. There was no way she could get him to turn over and eyeball her while she touched all that gorgeous male flesh!

She kept rubbing and kneading rhythmically, becoming mesmerized by her own actions, enjoying the sensual feel of his firm body under her oil-slick palms, the scent of lavender, chamomile, and male perspiration filled her nostrils. It was sexy voyeurism at its best! Rosy reveled in it. She couldn't remember the last time she'd so enjoyed a man's body. It felt naughty and wrong and yet so right! What was Benedict doing to her? She didn't care. She gave herself up to the moment and let the minutes stretch on and on.

Eventually a noise outside alerted Rosy to the time. She straightened and rotated her shoulders to ease the ache. Benedict just lay there. Quietly she went around to the head of the table. Benedict's eyes were shut, his breathing deep and regular. A soft smile tugged at Rosy's lips. Comatose! Let him sleep. She covered him lightly with a sheet and tiptoed out of the room.

Slowly the shades of sleep lifted as soft strains of music lapped around him. As he rose to consciousness, Benedict found he couldn't move. His body was infused with lethargy. It felt heavy and yet weightless at the same time. It took a huge amount of effort to crank open one eye. Where was he? He managed to crack open his other eye. In a pastel room with soft lighting. Ah, that's right. He'd been having a massage with Rosy.

The last thing he remembered was girding himself for her order to turn on his back and wondering how he'd cope with Rosy's puppy-brown eyes and satiny hands roving all over his body. He'd felt like a gauche teenager with hormones tearing around his bloodstream and pooling in his groin. But heck, in spite of all that, he must've fallen asleep. How long had he been out?

He eased himself upright and swung his legs over the table edge. He sat there, his limbs feeling deliciously relaxed. Boy, he hadn't felt so rested for ages. He flexed his fingers and toes to start the blood pumping. He wanted to lie back down and go to sleep. That massage had been something else. Rosy could give him a rub any time.

From outside the room, he could hear muted noises and smell the tantalizing aroma of roasted meat. His taste buds kicked in. Mmm, he was starving. It must be tea time.

Tea time?

Hell! He should have been back in Perth. He was meant to be going out for dinner. He'd never make it.

Benedict bounded off the bed, adrenaline suddenly pumping through his body. He needed a phone so he could ring Hovea and apologize.

No! He needed clothes first. He hopped about, trying to get into his jeans quickly. The oil made his skin sticky and his co-ordination was shot as his body was still in sleep mode and hadn't caught up with his brain. He got his foot caught in the wrong trouser leg and he knocked into the table, then into a chair until he finally managed to get into his jeans properly. He grabbed his shirt and thrust his arms into it, buttoning it as he went through the door into the living room, and on into the kitchen where Rosy and the boys were finishing their dinner.

'Sleep well, Laverton?' Rosy had heard him thumping about in the massage room and had schooled her face into a cool, bland mask so he wouldn't realize how much he had her rattled. She had to admit, it was a relief to see him dressed, even if his shirt buttons were done up in a haphazard fashion. He was much more manageable dressed than butt naked.

'Yes, thanks,' he said, still groggy from his deep sleep. 'What's the time?'

'Seven.'

'Seven! I've been asleep hours! You should have woken me!'

'You were sleeping like a baby. You obviously needed it. I did ring Martha to explain where you were, so she wouldn't worry.' Rosy nibbled on her lower lip. He didn't look too pleased. She turned to the children. 'You can leave the table, boys. Go and clean your teeth and hop into bed. I'll come and read you a story in a minute.' She glanced back at Benedict.

He raked his hand through his hair, making it peak boyishly. 'I should have been in Perth hours ago.'

'Oh.'

'I've got to go.'

'A hot date?' Now why did she ask that? Keep your mouth shut, Rosy Scott!

Benedict didn't immediately answer. Hot wasn't an adjective he'd have chosen to describe Hovea. He thought of her waiting for him in her cool, cream interior designed penthouse, with her immaculate, designer label clothes and flawless make up.

He looked at the butter yellow walls strewn with childish art and the slim woman in her sleeveless pink T-shirt and blue jeans, with her hair scraped back in a slightly cock-eyed ponytail. Dark tendrils stuck to her skin where she'd pushed the hair out of her eyes with oily hands. He knew whom he'd prefer to date, who was the hottest woman since vindaloo curry. Even though she was trying to appear coolly disassociated with him at this precise moment. He knew how hot Rosy could get. As for Hovea . . .

'She's not exactly a date,' he hedged.

'But it is a she?' Rosy wasn't surprised. Benedict was hunky, handsome, and single. Why wouldn't he have a woman waiting for him?

'She's a business associate.'

'Sounds grand.'

'And an old friend.'

'Even better.'

'Are you jealous?' Benedict liked the idea. He'd been jealous this afternoon. It was nice for the compliment to be reversed!

'No! How ridiculous. Why on earth would I be jealous? I hardly know you and we don't have that sort of relationship. Or any relationship, come to that!'

'We could try,' Benedict grinned. Jealousy meant she was interested.

'Never.'

'It would be fun.'

'It wouldn't.'

'How do you know unless you try?'

'Didn't you say you had to leave, Laverton?' She gave him an icy stare. It didn't faze him.

'Don't change the subject.'

'You were the one procrastinating after saying you had a hot date.'

'I didn't say it was hot. That was your interpretation. Once you meet Hovea, you'll understand that hot is not a word to describe her.'

Hovea! Rosy hated the woman already. For having a sophisticated name. For having a dinner date with Benedict. For being his business associate. And for being an old friend. How could Rosy compete? Hah! But did she want to? No, of course not. Hovea was welcome to him.

'I shan't be meeting her,' Rosy said.

'Course you will.'

'Very unlikely. We move in completely different circles.'

'But there's a common denominator.'

'What?' Rosy drew her brows together in a puzzled frown.

'Me.'

She threw back her head and laughed. 'You are not a common denominator, Laverton. You might be someone in this Hovea's life, but you're just passing through mine. Go back to the city and leave me alone.'

Benedict folded his arms across his chest. 'No,' he said and sounded as if he meant it.

'No?' Rosy managed to stop her jaw from hanging open. Just what was Laverton's problem? Why couldn't he disappear and leave her in peace? It was unnerving having him standing in her small kitchen, looking arrogant, dark, and handsome. She had to get shot of him. She'd had enough of his disturbing presence for one day.

'You have to go. For starters, you've got to ring Hovea and tell her your date is off,' she bluntly pointed out, rising to her feet and noisily stacking the dirty dishes.

Benedict grinned. 'Yes, I'd better. Can I use your phone?'

'If you must.' She gestured to the wall phone and carried on clattering the plates.

'Thanks.' Benedict sauntered over to the phone, covertly watching Rosy's jerky actions. Her whole body bristled with hostility. Hmm, interesting. He punched in some numbers and Hovea answered almost immediately.

'Hovea, it's Benedict. Yes, hi! Look, I shan't be able to make it tonight. Yes, I know. I'm sorry it's such short notice, but I'm still down south. No, nothing is wrong. Martha's fine. I've just got caught up unexpectedly.' His eyes traveled with appreciation down the rigid line of Rosy's back to her cute, taut bottom that curved so very nicely in her tight blue jeans. Yup, discovering the attractive Rosy Scott had been totally unexpected. 'I'll be back tomorrow. Yes, I'll ring you. Bye.'

Benedict replaced the receiver and leaned back on the counter to study Rosy. She was up to her elbows in suds and furiously scrubbing at a sauce pan. 'Thanks for that,' he said.

'You're welcome.' She didn't turn around, but kept on scrubbing.

'Now about Friday.'

'Friday?'

'And our date. Shall I pick you up about six?'

At this, Rosy did twist around. She opened and shut her mouth a couple of times. What was he going on about?

'There is no date,' she said and resolutely carried on washing up.

'You promised me an intimate dinner for two.'

'You don't really want to carry on with this, this circus,' said Rosy in exasperation.

'You promised me. I suffered the Laughing Duck for you.'

'That was part of the Bachelor Ball

deal. We've eaten another meal together since then.' She grabbed a tea towel that sported huge red poppies and began drying dishes.

'It wasn't intimate.'

'But the massage was,' she pointed out and then wished she hadn't. The hot fire in Benedict's eyes wasn't reassuring.

'It sure was,' grinned Benedict. 'I'm just annoyed with myself I fell asleep. Next time, I'll keep my eyes wide open.'

'There won't be a next time.' She'd blindfold him if there were!

Benedict's smile widened, as if he could read her mind. Rosy willed her cheeks not to burn. 'But you hadn't finished. There's still my front to do.'

Eek! In your dreams!

'Look,' said Rosy, trying not to think of his body under her hands and decided attack was the best form of defense. 'I have a heap of things to do and I'd appreciate it if you left.'

'I will once you agree to Friday night.'

'There's no where else to go but the Laughing Duck.'

'Let me worry about that.'

'And I'd need to find a babysitter.'

'If you get stuck, I'm sure my mother would oblige.'

'But you said she wasn't the maternal sort.'

Benedict shoved his hands into his pockets and rocked back on his heels. 'She won't cause irreparable psychological damage in a few hours of child minding.'

It was the laughter in his voice that made her weaken.

'Okay, deal,' she said and then shoved her hands into the cooling sudsy water so she didn't have to shake on it. She'd already touched Benedict far too much today.

9

Benedict bit into a fat, succulent king prawn and tried to stop his eyes from glazing over with boredom. The controlled, sophisticated woman sitting opposite him coolly dissected smoked salmon and forked minute, dainty portions into her mouth. Her coral lipstick was perfect, as was the rest of her chic make-up and clothes.

Benedict couldn't help but visualize Rosy, plowing her way through her pile of chips the size of Mount Kosciusko, talking around mouthfuls, spontaneous laughter spilling from her rose-bud lips and merriment lighting her dark eyes.

'Darling, you haven't heard a word I've said.' Hovea pouted and she clicked her long, pink-tipped fingernails against her frosted wine glass.

Benedict dragged himself away from the enchanting vision of Rosy. 'Sorry.

How's your lunch?'

'Nice,' she shrugged expressively. 'Though nothing outrageously special.'

Except for the price, Benedict silently countered. He wondered what Rosy's reaction would be to the over-priced gourmet food at one of Perth's most prestigious restaurants. And to the view. The Swan River stretched before them, a huge, gleaming aquamarine gem. Yachts and windsurfers danced across the rippled surface, sending the water slapping against the boardwalks where puff-chested pelicans and sleek black cormorants perched. He must bring her here.

'Benedict!'

'Yes?'

'You're miles away.'

'I've a lot on my mind.'

'So it seems. Do tell. Was your weekend simply horrendous?'

'No, far from it.' He didn't want to elaborate.

'You were dreading it.'

'Yes, but it exceeded expectations.'

'Oh?' Hovea cast him a speculative look. 'Did you meet anyone special?'

'I met a lot of my mother's new friends. What about your weekend? Did you go sailing as planned?' Benedict quickly deflected the conversation. He didn't want to invite her cynical slant on what had proved to be a highly entertaining time. For all his teasing that Rosy would meet Hovea, Benedict had no intention of introducing the two women.

Hovea nodded. 'Yes, of course, I did. Why wouldn't I? But you were missed dreadfully. They all wanted to know where you where and what you were doing. They were terribly sympathetic. At least you won't have to go rustic again for a while.'

Next weekend, actually. But Benedict didn't enlighten her. Instead, he asked questions about the sailing and Hovea furnished him with a lightly humorous account of the weekend. Originally, Benedict had been annoyed to cancel his berth on the yacht, but his mother had been adamant that she'd needed him for the weekend. Now, he harbored no regrets.

Hovea took a delicate sip of her dry white wine. She put her elbows on the snowy white tablecloth and peaked her fingers in a steeple, giving Benedict a long, thoughtful scrutiny.

Benedict regarded her through his lashes as he finished his seafood platter. Now what was Hovea up to? He distrusted that calculated expression in her eyes.

'Benedict, darling, there's something important I want to ask you.'

'Yes?' he said warily.

'We've known each other a long time.'

'Yes. Ten years or more.'

'And we know each other well.'

'Yes. As well as anybody.' His wariness increased.

'And we're fond of each other.'

It cranked up further. Where was all this leading? Benedict's survival instincts bristled to red alert. Hovea never said anything without a good reason. She was one tough cookie for all her fragile looks.

'We're both intelligent people,' she swept along, not waiting for his reply. 'We're both single and not getting any younger.'

Benedict experienced a blast of panic. She was going to propose to him! How appalling! He couldn't imagine being married to Hovea. Everything would be too controlled and stark. His mind swung to a brilliant yellow kitchen with paper plate and macaroni creations stuck on every available surface, potted herbs in the window, shoes and toys scattered over the floor, and Henry the hairy dog asleep on the step.

Hovea smoothed a non-existent strand of hair into place and opened her deep azure eyes wide at Benedict. Sweat prickled his brow and upper lip. This was awful — embarrassing. He took a hasty swig of red wine. It was a smooth, rich vintage, one of the best and far superior to the Laughing Duck's liquor. But at this precise moment it tasted worse than that establishment's house red. It resembled vinegar.

'Sweetie,' said Hovea. 'I want to have your baby.'

The wine lodged in Benedict's throat. It took immense effort not to spray it out over the cool beautiful blonde sitting opposite him. He choked and swallowed with difficulty, wiping his eyes from the effort.

She was kidding, right?

One glance at Hovea's expectant face and he knew with a dreadful sinking sensation she wasn't. Hell. Benedict decided to chance another swig. Hang it all, he drained the glass. That was better. No it wasn't! Hovea was still calmly regarding him like a hungry crocodile would a boat full of tourists.

Hovea laughed. 'I see I've surprised you.'

Benedict shook his head in an attempt to clear it. 'Surprised is an understatement. Did you just say what I thought you said?'

'It makes sense, darling. Our joint gene pool would be marvelous. Any child we created would be beautiful, intelligent, and blessed with all the advantages money could buy.'

Benedict immediately thought of a small, dark version of himself, but with a wild cowlick of hair. It was replaced with the image of a little girl with brown pigtails and the largest, puppy-dog brown eyes imaginable. Blonde, blue-eyed children didn't rate at all.

Hold on a moment! He'd never envisaged having any children. It had always been an issue he'd rather not explore. He'd never consciously imagined his own children and now he had little people with cowlicks and pigtails burned on his brain. He tried to shunt them away to a far recess in his brain so he could concentrate on Hovea's outlandish suggestion.

'I'm not embarrassed that my biological clock is ticking. It has been for a while. But with my corporate life style, it's hard to meet a man.'

'Come off it, Hovea, you're surrounded by men at work and you've dated lots of them.'

'Not that many.' She gave a girlish laugh that was at odds with her powerful persona. 'And you were *always* my favorite, Benedict.'

If Benedict didn't know better, he would have sworn Hovea batted her eyelashes at him. But that wasn't her style. It suddenly struck him that he didn't know her well at all or he would have seen this coming. He had always thought Hovea lacked a biological clock of any variety and that was why she was usually an undemanding companion. She'd never shown the slightest interest in marriage and babies. Had never revealed a maternal bent. Benedict tugged at his collar. 'I'm not ready to settle down,' he protested.

'Darling,' Hovea gave a tinkling laugh. 'I'm not expecting you to marry me. We can have joint custody of the child. I'll arrange all the day care and nanny side of things. You won't have to do a thing. Except, of course, the main thing.' She sounded almost coy.

Yuck!

Benedict inwardly shuddered. This was all so clinical. 'If ever I have children, I want to be a proper dad.'

Now where had those words come from? He'd never harbored a dream to be a proper dad!

'And you will be, darling. You can take him to the park or skiing or sailing or whatever one does with little ones. Anyway, I know it's all a bit sudden. But give it some serious thought. I'm sure you want an heir to your empire. I know I do. I'd rather go about it the old fashioned way than opt for a donor.'

'There is nothing remotely old fashioned in what you're suggesting.'

'If you want marriage, Benedict, I'm prepared to do that too.'

The hairs on the back of his neck rose skyward at the suggestion. 'Gee, thanks,' he said, not believing this was really happening to him. Up until the auction, Benedict had never considered children and families. Now, all of a sudden, he wanted a relationship with a divorcee with kids, and yet was being railroaded to father someone else's child.

Hovea laughed girlishly again. Benedict wished she wouldn't. It brought him out in a cold sweat. He couldn't trust her when she did that.

'We'll talk about it again in a while,' said Hovea. 'Now what shall we have for dessert?'

Babies one moment, dessert the next? Benedict was reeling. What sort of woman was she? Maybe early menopause was making her mind wander? No! He wouldn't go there.

'I can tell you now, the answer is no,' he said.

'What? No baby or no sorbet?' Hovea smiled.

'No to a baby. It would never work.'

'Of course it would.' Hovea gave her tinkling laugh. It set Benedict's teeth on edge, like grapefruit after toothpaste, and sent another rush of shivers down his spine. 'It's just down to mind set. Once you've given it some thought, you'll realize my suggestion is imminently practical. You and I are of the same ilk, Benedict. We don't need to get bogged down in all the romantic stuff. We're way beyond all that soppiness now. We can be cool and clear-headed about it. Anyway, darling, don't make a snap decision. Sleep on it. Now, for more pressing decisions. I think I'll have the lemon cream.'

★   ★   ★

Rosy tugged down the hem of her red dress for the umpteenth time, but it made no difference to the amount of thigh she displayed. To say she had cold feet was putting it mildly, and they weren't only cold because of the amount of sheer stocking-clad leg she had exposed when sliding into the close confines of Benedict's Jaguar. No, it was the whole thing: a date with Stud Laverton, sans children.

Benedict had turned up on the dot of seven, ready for their so-called 'proper date'. He'd looked cool and in control, where as she'd felt like a jellyfish in a blender. As she'd tottered towards his car on her borrowed high heels, Rosy was resigned that there was no going back: it was crunch time.

She fussed with the hem again. She had no idea the dress would ride so high. Another twitch and her knickers would be on display! She'd kill Janice for talking her into wearing it. It was nothing more than a knee brace masquerading as a dress.

She felt totally out of her depth. What on earth did Laverton have to prove taking her out on this ridiculous farce of a date? He had a perfectly good girlfriend keeping the home fires burning in Perth. He didn't need to go through with all these shenanigans with her. There was no point to it.

It was nerve-racking having him so close to her. His arm was a breath away. She could feel the sex appeal rolling off him in waves. It made her very, very nervous. And very, very hot!

Yup, this whole date thing was a bad, bad idea.

'Okay?' Benedict interrupted Rosy's troubled thoughts, slanting her a smile that was as hard to resist as the rest of him. To do him justice, his eyes remained firmly on her face and ignored the tangle of slim, almost bare limbs under his nose. Rosy wouldn't have blamed him if he had taken a quick squiz. The damn dress invited men to drool, for goodness sake! Really, what had Janice been thinking to suggest she wear it? And what the hell had she been thinking to agree? She must have rocks in her head.

'Fine, thanks.' Rosy gave another nervous tug at her hem. Benedict's eyes flickered.

'Nice dress,' he said. There was a ghost of a laugh in his voice.

'Hmph! It's all a matter of taste. I was going to wear my posh frock, but it had a stain on it. I could have worn my brown one, but I was out maneuvered by Janice.' And the dog. How on earth had Henry managed to pull it into his basket and cover it with yellow hair? If she didn't know any better, she'd have said there had been a conspiracy afoot.

'I'm glad, if the brown dress you're alluding to is the dowdy thing you wore at the ball.'

Rosy frowned. Benedict smiled enigmatically and started the car. It rolled away from the verge in a powerful, smooth surge.

Her brown dress wasn't that bad, whatever anyone said. Rosy huffed and crossed her arms tightly across her chest. She immediately regretted the action, as her hemline shot north and her breasts almost broke free from the flimsy scarlet boob tube. She hastily uncrossed her arms and made a grab at the skirt. With her other hand, she wriggled the tube to a more modest level. She did a mental eye roll. She wasn't going to survive the night clothed at this rate. How did anyone wear such a dress without becoming a twitching wreck? Janice had a lot to answer for. She sometimes took too much on herself. She was overdue having stern words with her friend.

Benedict grinned. Rosy saw it in the green gleam of the dashboard lights. She felt a surge of panic. Perhaps this evening wasn't going to be as uncompli- cated as she'd thought. She'd reckoned there were only a handful of places where Benedict could take her for a meal. There weren't that many restaurants and hotels in the area. Probably three or four and all about forty minutes away. She'd thought the evening was going to be relatively safe.

Until the dress and the smug expression on his face.

She looked out of the window. They were heading out of town, towards the tip.

The tip?

Rosy nibbled her lower lip and frowned. 'Where are we going?'

'You'll see.' His enigmatic smile

widened a smidge.

Rosy nibbled some more. 'But this is the way to the rubbish dump. There's nothing else on this road.'

'Have faith, my sweet.'

Rosy squirmed on the brown leather seat. It was all very well for him to say, but she liked to be in control. Heading toward the tip in this stupid dress and with this dangerous man made her hyperventilate. She continued to stare out of the window for inspiration, trying to work out what Benedict Laverton was up to. They passed a sign with an airplane on it and Rosy's head whipped around. Airplane? That's right, the airstrip was out this way too. It was used by owners of small planes and the Royal Flying Doctor. Lord! They weren't going to fly somewhere? Good grief, that possibility hadn't even occurred to her.

Rosy clenched her hands and then forced herself to relax, stretched out each finger, one by one, and flexed them against her knees. Of course they wouldn't be flying. Ridiculous. People like her didn't fly off for a dinner date. Okay, so people like Benedict might. But surely he would have said something. Wouldn't he?

Benedict swung the Jaguar through the airstrip gates. Rosy immediately clenched her hands into tight fists. There were no planes in sight. But that was a small relief. Because there was a big, black helicopter and Benedict was heading the Jag straight for it.

'What are you doing?' Rosy squeaked in consternation.

'Your carriage awaits, Princess.' Benedict smiled. Rosy saw the self-satisfied gleam in his eyes and felt a surge of anger tinged with a healthy dose of fear.

'I'm not going in that death machine!'

Benedict's eyes narrowed. 'That is no death machine. That is a state of the art helicopter which flies like a bird.'

'Forget it! I'm not going in it, bird or no bird.'

'Why?'

'Because . . . ? Just because!'

'Not scared are you, Rosy?'

Petrified, but she wouldn't admit it. Not to him. She had her pride. 'Don't be ridiculous.'

'Then prove it. Get in.' Benedict slid out of his seat before she could argue and tossed the car keys to a young man dressed in black and silver coveralls. 'Hi, Tom. Is she all ready to go?'

'Yes, Mr. Laverton. She's running sweet.'

'Good.'

'You'll call when you're ready to be collected?'

'Will do. Thanks, Tom. You fit, Ms. Scott?'

Rosy stood to one side shivering. 'I don't know about this, Laverton.'

'It'll be fine. Come on, I'll help you in.'

'What's wrong with the Laughing Duck? They do great pizzas.'

'You're kidding, right?'

'I've never been more serious.' She hugged her arms around her trembling body.

'You are scared. Haven't you flown

213

before? Is that it?' She gave him her best glacial stare. Benedict threw back his head and laughed. 'Boy! Have I got a treat for you. You'll love it, Rosy. There's something about flying that's exhilarating.'

'I like my feet firmly on the ground, thanks.' And they hadn't been since Benedict Laverton had stormed into her life.

'That's the trouble with you, you're scared to feel the heights, to try new things, experience the rush of daring exploits. Good thing I'm around. I can unfetter your wings and help you soar to the heavens.'

Rosy gave an unladylike snort. 'You are not 'around', Laverton. Our relationship, such as it is, finishes right after this dinner date. There won't be any soaring or unfettering of any sort and the sooner you realize that the better.'

'Well, darling, I think at this precise moment, you're doing the unfettering all by yourself.' Benedict looked pointedly at her dress. Rosy immediately glanced down. Her cleavage was barely covered. Benedict took advantage of her sudden confusion and swept her up in his arms and deposited her in the passenger seat of the helicopter. Rosy gasped her outrage while trying to keep the stretchy red fabric from concentrating into a fat bunch around her midriff and leaving everything else bare.

'You can't do this to me!'

'I just did.' Benedict snapped her seat belt in place, ignoring her slaps as she tried to undo it.

'But what if we crash?' she wailed, realizing she was losing the battle.

'We won't. I'm a good pilot.'

'You're flying this thing?' Her voice rose to the highest note on the keyboard.

'Yep. Exciting, eh?'

'I think I'm going to be sick.'

'Bags are in the back.'

'You're unfeeling.'

'No, practical.' He glanced over to her as he settled himself more comfortably into the pilot seat. Rosy tried to look brave and confident. She must have failed because his expression softened.

'Just sit back and enjoy the trip, sweetheart. I promise you, I'll be careful. Conditions are as good as they get and you should have a fantastic first ride.'

'You should have warned me.' She tried not to sound sulky, but real fear undermined her natural buoyancy.

'I wanted to surprise you.'

She gave a short, troubled laugh that sounded more like a sob. 'I hate surprises. They usually spell trouble.'

Like the time she found out she was pregnant, so she and Steve had to get married.

Like the time she found Steve in bed with her best friend.

Like the time she found his note saying he'd gone for good and taken her housekeeping money.

Of course, she couldn't forget the time she went to the bank and found he'd cleaned out not just her purse, but their joint account too.

'I much prefer to be in control.'

Benedict went through the pre-flight check, but twisted in his seat to face

216

her. 'I don't blame you for feeling that way. You've had a pretty poor trot, haven't you, honey?'

His sudden tenderness lodged a lump of tears in her throat. She madly tried to swallow them and hated the weakness he inspired in her. 'No!' It came out a strangled croak.

'Rosy, from what I can make out about your life, you've had to struggle on your own for a long time.'

'You've been gossiping about me!' She was outraged. She didn't want him to know the gory details of her past. She'd left it all behind. She was a good provider and homemaker for her boys. She didn't need to rely on anyone anymore. And more than anything else, she didn't want his pity.

'It was all given freely, I didn't have to ask. Your friends are concerned about you.' He chuckled. 'And they want to make sure my intentions toward you are of the purest kind. It's cute.'

'Cute?' Yuck!

'That they care so much.'

Rosy nibbled her fingertip. Did she really want to ask this next question or would she be better off keeping her mouth shut? But what were his intentions? She'd really like to know because he was wreaking a great deal of havoc. She couldn't sleep, didn't want to eat, and her mind was permanently preoccupied. Even hard, long, nighttime runs around the silent streets didn't exercise their usual relief from stress.

But the next instant, any questions she had went completely out of her mind. Benedict had started the helicopter.

She froze as the helicopter engines roared into life. Her fingers convulsed around the miniscule hem of her dress and she clamped her knees tightly together to stop them shaking. Benedict glanced at her and then paused in his pre-flight check. She really was scared and not just hamming it up to prevent them from going as he'd presumed. He reached over and covered her white-knuckled hands with his to reassure her.

It had the opposite effect. Rosy jumped two-foot in the air and squeaked. Her face flamed the same color as her scarlet dress. She scowled at him.

'Relax,' he said.

'Can't.'

'It'll be a blast. You'll love it.'

'You're not taking me seriously here, Laverton. I-do-NOT-want-to-fly!'

'You're being too negative and intense. Think of something to take your mind off it.'

'What?'

'This . . . ' Suddenly, Benedict's mouth was on hers and all her fear of flying shattered to smithereens as his lips and tongue worked their amazing magic on her. Her blood went fizz and pop, working through her veins like champagne. Flying was a doodle compared to kissing Benedict Laverton! She brought up her hand to shove him away. But somehow, instead of pushing, her hand was gliding upwards across his chest, over his shoulders, and through his short, dark hair, clutching hold of it and tugging him closer into the kiss. It went on and on. Utter heaven!

Benedict groaned against her mouth, 'I can't do this, Rosy. These damn seats weren't designed for necking.'

Necking? Is that what she'd just been doing? Yes! Lord, she completely lost it around this man. He made her act out of character and she loved it. Sort of. 'Not that I wouldn't like to continue this someplace more comfy,' he said, his voice low and sexy.

'Good idea. Let's go back to my place.' Hers sounded high and panicky in comparison.

Benedict paused, considering. 'But you might chicken out once we got there and make some excuse about the boys,' he said.

'Sometimes you have to take gambles in life. Aren't you interested?' Rosy ran a finger down the front of his crisp white shirt and smiled with what she hoped was wantonness. If she could get him home, she wouldn't have to fly. At least not in the helicopter!

Benedict crushed her hand in his bigger one and held it against his fast beating heart. 'Darling, I'm very interested, more than you probably realize, but I promised you a night out on the town.'

'You coerced me, you mean.'

'Same thing,' he glinted at her. 'And I'm going to deliver.'

Rosy blew out a long breath and hugged her arms around her body. 'Let's get it over and done with then.'

'You don't sound keen.'

'I'm not.'

'At least you're honest.' Benedict softly laughed and all Rosy's cells glowed at the warmth of his tone. She bravely ignored the reaction. It would never do. In a few seconds it was a past memory, because all her concentration was on the helicopter as it became airborne. She screwed up her eyes and bit her bottom lip. She kept her eyes closed for a good ten minutes and only opened them when Benedict said, 'It's okay, princess, you can breathe again.

221

Just take a look. Isn't it magnificent?'

The day was dying in a fanfare of glory. The sun was throwing out its last rays and turning the sky a bruised purple, lavender, gold, orange, and scarlet. It would have been fantastic if Rosy hadn't felt so flipping terrified. The terror intensified as the town melted away and the helicopter gained height. Rosy did her best to look out the window and admire the view. But, along with her taut nerves, her rolling stomach robbed her of any enjoyment.

'Where are we going?' she asked after a while, trying to control the nervous tremor in her voice.

'Perth.'

'Perth! You must be kidding. That's miles away.'

'It won't take long in this bird.'

'But I'll be too far away from the children. What if they need me?'

'I've got my mobile phone. Janice will ring if there's a problem. Relax. You deserve a treat.'

Rosy fumed. He kept telling her to

relax. But how could she? She was scared witless and with every air mile she became more so. She tried to count her breaths, count backwards from a hundred in Italian, and recite poems she'd learned at school. Anything to keep her travel sickness at bay. It worked. But by the time Benedict landed the helicopter, Rosy felt decidedly queasy and weak-kneed.

Benedict had arranged for a taxi to pick them up from the foreshore helipad and within minutes he was ushering her into one of the city's most prestigious restaurants. Rosy almost backed out. The clientele shrieked of money. Women wore dresses that, taken singularly, would have constituted her monthly food bill. The food looked like something out of a glossy gourmet magazine.

Rosy felt totally out-classed, while Benedict fit in perfectly.

'I'll order you a brandy,' said Benedict with concern. 'You look awfully pale.'

'I'll be okay in a minute. If you'll excuse me, I'll go and freshen up.'

Benedict had heard that one before. His eyes narrowed. 'You won't run out on me this time?' he said.

'Hey, look at me, I'm not running anywhere.'

10

Rosy wobbled toward the rest rooms and sagged thankfully against the peach porcelain vanity unit. She stared at her haggard face. So much for tizzying herself up. The red dress made her look a hundred times worse. It emphasized the waxy whiteness of her cheeks and the feverish glitter of her eyes.

She took a paper cup from the dispenser for a couple of gulps of icy water. Big mistake. Her stomach rebelled and, in an instant, she was hanging over the toilet bowl. At least afterwards she felt a little better, slightly more human, and a lot less like rubber. She resumed her position at the vanity unit and, after rinsing out her mouth, began to repair the damage to her make-up.

There was another woman in the room. A cool looking blonde wearing an expensive lilac silk suit that screamed designer label. She stared at Rosy with an intenseness that bordered on rude. Rosy guessed she was in the woman's way and obligingly shunted along the unit a little so they could both share the mirror. As Rosy touched up her lipstick, the woman said, 'Didn't you come with Benedict Laverton?'

'Yes.' Rosy waited, watching the woman expertly slick deep plum-colored gloss on her own lips and spray on a delicate scent behind each diamond-studded, perfect shell-like ear.

'Are you a friend of Benedict's or a business acquaintance?' asked the woman as she smoothed an immaculate eyebrow with her finger.

That was a difficult question to answer. Rosy hadn't quite defined her relationship with Benedict. Common sense told her there wasn't one, but instinct said otherwise. There was definitely something between them that wouldn't go away. She hesitated.

'A friend,' she said finally. After all,

he had rolled about in her back garden, read to her children, and eaten at her table.

And kissed her senseless!

'Ah,' said the woman.

Rosy detected an ocean of significance in that one syllable, but wasn't quite sure what it was.

'I'm Rosy Scott,' she offered, trying to be friendly.

'He's never mentioned you.' The woman's brow puckered delicately. 'At least, I don't recall him saying anything.'

'No reason to.'

'But I know all Benedict's close friends.'

'Ah.' It was Rosy's turn for one, significant syllable. She disliked this woman's attitude. What had she done to offend her?

'My name's Hovea Clarke.' The woman held out her hand. Rosy took it. It was cool and firm.

So this was Hovea, the hot date. She was exactly as Rosy imagined — tall, attractive, and reeked of sophistication. And she suited Benedict admirably. She was much more his sort than Rosy in her borrowed red dress and cheap make-up.

'Pleased to meet you, Hovea, and I have heard of you.'

Hovea smiled with condescension. 'I'm sure you have, Rosy. I'm one of his oldest friends.' She paused for an artfully dramatic moment and then said, 'He's probably told you I'm going to have his baby.'

The room spun, the walls caved in, and then receded. Rosy clutched hold of the basin for support as her heart hit the ground and shattered. She suddenly felt very, very sick again.

'No! No, he hasn't said a thing,' she managed to force out through the intense tightening of her throat. 'But then, we're not that close.'

'It's all very exciting,' said Hovea with another condescending twist of her lips.

'I'm sure it is.' Rosy was desperate to

end this humiliation. 'Congratulations. I hope the pregnancy goes well.' What else could she say? 'I'd best get back to Benedict.' She didn't want to, but there was no alternative. She was stuck with the two-timing skunk for the rest of the evening. But she realized in a flash that she didn't have to suffer alone. 'Do feel free to join us, Hovea. I'm sure Benedict would be delighted to see you.'

Rosy's legs had morphed to rubber. How she made it back to their table, she had no idea. But as soon as she did, Rosy picked up the brandy and slung it back in one hit. She welcomed the burning sensation as the rich amber liquid slid down her tense throat and scorched a straight trail to the pit of her empty stomach. But she hadn't reckoned on the kickback of neat alcohol. She coughed, spluttered, and had to suffer the ignobility of Benedict thumping her on the back and giving her his crisp, white linen handkerchief to mop her eyes.

'Take it easy, Rosy,' laughed Benedict. 'That's no way to drink vintage brandy.'

'I don't know. It had the desired affect. Can I have another one?' She croaked. She desperately needed it. She'd been so fooled by Benedict's character. He was such a charmer and such a snake! Hitting on her while another woman carried his child.

'Of course, but I think you should sip the next one.'

'Don't tell me what to do, Laverton!' Already the brandy fired her blood and fueled the rage inside her. She felt ready to explode and had to exercise great self-control not to bawl him out in front of all these up-market diners in this posh Perth restaurant and then walk out in a blaze of glory. She snatched up a still warm sesame seed roll from a basket and proceeded to murder it between her fingers, crumbling it over her gold rimmed, white side plate.

Benedict sat back in his chair and regarded her warily. 'Are you feeling okay?'

'Never better.' The brandy was served and Rosy went to sling it back, had second thoughts, and took a small sip. She still had to get through this travesty and home. There were still hours to endure.

'I thought you'd like this place,' said Benedict, attempting to lighten the suddenly frigid atmosphere between them. 'It's one of my favorite restaurants. The food is excellent and there's a great view of the city and river.'

'You take too much upon yourself. You thought I'd like to fly, too.'

'That was a big mistake. Sorry. It's just I love flying so much, I thought you would too.'

'And I suppose you ordered for me as well?'

'Ah,' Benedict sucked in his lower lip. 'I did. You were taking a while in the ladies room and I thought you'd probably only want something light to settle your stomach. But I did something wrong, didn't I?'

'Yes! No! Oh, damn!' Tears shimmered

suddenly in her eyes. She'd been stupid to think he was different. She'd tried hard not to like him, but it was difficult. He had appeared so nice. He was funny, attractive, and good with the boys. And he was so damn sexy! She'd been seduced by his dark eyes and dimpled smile, while all the time he was like Steve. Like Rick.

'Rosy, sweetheart, what's wrong? Look, if you're feeling too ill, I'll take you home.' Benedict reached for her hand and she pulled it away, snatching up the brandy glass instead.

'I'm fine. Don't fuss.' Leave me alone and allow me some dignity.

He sighed. 'Here comes our meal. Re-order if it's not to your liking.'

The waiter placed a delicate china bowl of chicken soup in front of Rosy. 'No, this looks wonderful,' she said, and found she meant it when the delicious aroma swirled around her, tantalizing her taste buds.

They ate in silence for a few moments. The soup did much to revive

Rosy. She was still wildly mad with Benedict, but at least she didn't feel so ill now. She kept her eyes pinned on the creamy, champagne-colored soup so she wouldn't have to look at him. She knew he watched her, could feel him trying to gauge her mood. He was no doubt waiting for the opportunity to say something sexy and flirtatious to put her in the right mood for seduction. He'd have a long, long wait. Eternity wouldn't be long enough.

'I've mucked up, haven't I?' said Benedict, breaking the taut silence. 'I really wanted this night to be special.'

'Don't worry about it, Laverton. We can put it behind us as a never-to-be-repeated farce.'

'That's a bit strong.'

'Is it?' Rosy hissed. 'I should never have come with you. You should have stuck to your original plan — paid for the bachelor bid and then shot through.'

'What's brought this on? I thought we were getting on wonderfully.' His fingers curled around her wrist and his thumb rubbed backwards and forwards over the tender inner skin. Of course, it made her blood sing and Rosy felt like gnashing her teeth in frustration. He only had to touch her to cause heart failure! It was so unfair! Why him?

'I'm not denying there's a certain something,' she conceded.

'Chemistry.'

'Well, okay, chemistry. But it's not enough. I'm not going to become one of your women.'

'You flatter me, but I don't have a whole lot of women.' Benedict smiled with a tinge of bewilderment. 'Where did you get that idea from?'

'It's general knowledge,' Rosy hedged, squirming a little in her seat. She didn't want him to know she'd been reading up on his exploits in back issues of the magazines she'd raided from the hospital's waiting room. 'And I just met your girlfriend. I can't believe you'd be so arrogant as to bring me to the same restaurant she frequents. Your gall astounds me.'

'My girlfriend?' Benedict frowned and looked really confused.

'Here she comes now.'

Benedict followed Rosy's gaze. 'Hovea! Oh, God, what's she doing here?'

'That's not a very flattering thing to say about your girlfriend.'

'You don't know Hovea,' he said with feeling.

'While you certainly do.' Benedict shot a puzzled glance at Rosy. But before he could ask her to explain herself, Hovea descended on them. A cloud of her expensive perfume wafted over them.

'Benedict, darling!'

'Hovea.' He stood and politely kissed her cheek, while Rosy regarded Benedict with banked hostility. There was nothing remotely lover-like about his response to this beautiful woman. Rosy almost felt sorry for her. But she felt more sorry for herself. 'I understand you've already met Rosy,' Benedict said.

'Yes, we had a nice girlie chat earlier. I told her about the baby.'

'Baby?'

'I thought Portia if it was a girl and Rupert if a boy. What do you think?'

'Baby!' Good Lord, no wonder Rosy was spitting mad and had shot back the brandy so fast. He felt like doing the same! 'I think you'd better sit down, Hovea. Or are you with someone?' said Benedict, attempting to take charge of the situation. He had to put things right with Rosy. He didn't want her going off half-cocked with the wrong impression about Hovea and himself.

'Only a business associate and his wife. They left a few minutes ago. So do you like the names?'

'No.'

'Oh, I don't know, Benedict, I think they're very appropriate,' said Rosy.

'Thank you, Rosy, but there is no baby.'

'Oh, Benedict!' said Hovea, with such obvious affection Rosy cringed inside and wished herself a million miles away. 'You're not in denial, are you?'

'Hovea, drop the subject!' said

236

Benedict through clenched teeth.

'Don't be so stuffy, darling. She doesn't mind us discussing the baby. Do you, Rosy?' Rosy shook her head. 'See? Good. Now, I did want to clear up the baby's name. I want it to have my surname. Is that a problem?'

'It's not a problem, because there is no baby!'

Rosy looked from Benedict to Hovea and back again. This was confusing. Surely a sophisticated woman like Hovea wouldn't lie about having a baby? She was talking about it quite openly in a public place where anyone could overhear and she was obviously radiant at the prospect of motherhood. Her eyes were bright. Her cheeks were flushed. It just didn't make sense.

But Benedict lying about it did.

Men, in Rosy's experience, often lied to protect themselves. She knew her experience was limited, but not that limited. She just didn't know if she wanted to give Benedict the benefit of the doubt.

'Are you getting married?' she asked quietly.

'No!' said Benedict.

'Yes,' said Hovea at the same time. She looked at Benedict reproachfully. 'You said on Tuesday you wanted to.'

'I did not! I said I wanted to be a proper dad. And I said nothing about fathering your children! Damn it, Hovea, this is your agenda. It has nothing to do with me.'

'I don't know, Laverton,' said Rosy, her voice sweet as sugared arsenic. 'It sounds to me that you're very much involved. I think it's you who's in denial here.'

'Butt out, Rosy.'

She gave a hollow laugh as Hovea said, 'It's going to be brilliant having this child.'

'Why stop at one?' said Rosy. 'Have a pigeon pair.'

'Thank you, Rosy, now quit it!' Benedict glared at her and she stifled another humorless laugh. Not that she wanted to laugh. She shook her head in

238

despair. All she really wanted to do was walk away from this dreadful situation and give way to her unhappiness somewhere private.

'Oh, no,' said Hovea. 'One would be sufficient. I only need one.' Rosy closed her eyes. She didn't understand these people. They lived in a different world, a world where they ordered children like a commodity. Where were the essential ingredients of love and commitment?

'You should have at least two for company. While you're at it, Laverton, maybe I should order a couple too, to swell our footy team?' she said with an edge of sarcasm.

'It'd be my pleasure!' he shot back. 'Name the time and place!'

'Hah!' said Rosy. 'In your dreams.'

'Definitely. But what if we have girls?'

'Get real, Laverton.' But she tried not to squirm and blush at the thought of their girls, of having his babies. But it wouldn't happen! Not in a million years.

'With your genes, our daughters would be the super stars of the squad.' There was no mistaking the warmth in his voice, but she angrily blocked his words. While they were flattering and seductive, she would resist his charm and remember the issue here, which was Hovea's baby.

Luckily she was saved from replying by the interruption of a young, gushy woman with curly blonde hair and large, startling blue eyes which could only be through artificial means in Rosy's estimation.

'Hovea! Benedict! Lovely to see you. It's been an absolute age!' she said. There were a lot of cheek clashing and air kissing.

Benedict rolled his eyes in frustration and then caught Rosy's expression. She believed Hovea! Her anger hummed between them. It was a live, tangible thing and made more terrible because he couldn't redeem himself while in the busy restaurant. He needed to get her alone so he could convince her he was

240

telling the truth.

The blonde was introduced and then sat down between Benedict and Rosy. 'So what's the goss?' she said.

'We were just discussing Benedict's babies,' said Rosy. There was an edge to her voice that made Benedict wince it was so sharp. 'Hovea's having one and I might order a couple too.'

Benedict choked on his fruit juice. 'Hovea is not pregnant,' he said, but the women weren't listening. They were chattering excitedly. At least the blonde and Hovea were. Rosy was tight-lipped and silent.

'Cool,' the blonde was saying. 'I wouldn't mind having some too.'

Some? Benedict loosened his collar. This was worse than the bachelor auction. 'Hey, ladies!' he said, trying to take control of the situation.

'How many?' asked Rosy. She was enjoying herself, in an awful, terribly masochistic sort of way. She would make Benedict pay for the pain he was causing her, even if, in the process, she caused herself more grief.

'Six.'

Six!

'How about it, Stud?' said Rosy, ignoring his hunted look. If he couldn't take the heat, he shouldn't play with fire!

'Cut it out, Rosy.'

'I don't think you're taking this seriously,' said Hovea, frowning at Rosy.

'I'm taking it seriously,' said Benedict, 'And I'm telling you women now, for the record, I'm not available to populate Perth. Find some other poor bloke to do it!'

'Not up to it, Stud?' said Rosy.

She still didn't believe him! Self-righteous anger roared through Benedict's blood stream. 'I'll deal with you later, Rosy Scott!'

'You won't get the chance.' Rosy suddenly stood up, responding to his anger. He had no right to be furious. She was the one who'd been duped. He might think she was a simple country chick ready for the plucking, but she hadn't survived Steve's betrayal without gaining some savvy. 'Thanks for the meal. I'll find my own way home. Bye, ladies. Nice meeting you.'

Benedict couldn't believe it. 'You can't go,' he said, also rising to his feet.

'Watch me.' Rosy picked up her bag and jacket, held them tightly in her hand, and tried not to shake with all the suppressed emotion boiling inside her. 'And don't try to stop me.'

With her back ramrod straight and trying not to slip in her high heels, Rosy managed to make it across the dining room to the reception desk. She ordered a taxi. It would be hellishly expensive, but there was no way she was going home with Benedict. It was a good job the boys were sleeping over with Janice because it was going to be one very late night.

'Rosy!' Benedict was right behind her. He took hold of her arm. Her skin scorched at his touch, tremors rocketed straight to her belly and formed a whirlpool of tension there. She pulled her arm away. Her body might respond to him, but her brain would not! 'I'll take you home,' he said.

'No!'

'I'll drive you if you don't want to fly, but we need to talk.'

'You might need to, but I don't. There's been enough information shared tonight to satisfy me a long time. I don't want you anywhere near me, Laverton. The debt's clear now. We don't have to see each other again. Ever.'

'There is no baby!'

That's what Steve had said when Rosy heard rumors of him fathering someone else's baby. She'd been more trusting then. She'd believed him. Later, she'd discovered his duplicity. Her ex-best friend was pregnant. It had broken her heart and she wasn't game to go through the pain again.

'I don't want to see you again.' She was angry to hear her voice crack. She didn't want Benedict to know how much he'd hurt her.

'Believe me!'

She stared at him, felt the same dead despair Steve had caused all those years ago, and knew it was beyond her. How could she trust him, believe him?

'I can't,' she said starkly. 'Good bye, Benedict.'

11

'We're here, Miss.' Rosy started awake at the taxi driver's voice. How long had she been asleep? She was stiff, groggy, and totally disorientated. She tumbled out of the car and clutched her thin linen jacket close as the chilly night assaulted her.

She gasped and her heart skittered as a large, dark shape loomed from her front porch. 'I'll settle the fare,' said Benedict, his voice loud and harsh in the frosty air. The shock of seeing him rendered Rosy speechless. She hadn't expected him to follow her back and his presence was unnerving. Panic began to swirl in the pit of her stomach. What did he want that was so important to fly three hundred kilometers to see her in the dead of night?

'Thanks, mate.' The driver told him an astronomical figure. Rosy shut her eyes in horror. How much? Lord, how many massages would she have to give to afford that?

As the taillights of the taxi disappeared, Rosy shivered in earnest. She felt small and vulnerable, standing there with Benedict in only her short dress and jacket, her shoes dangling from the fingers of one hand.

'You must be freezing,' said Benedict. 'Let's get you inside.'

'You're not coming in!' she managed to hiss, clouds of frozen vapor forming around her.

'Rosy . . . '

'No way!' Her shivers became more pronounced and her teeth began to chatter.

'We have to talk.'

'There's nothing to say.'

'Like hell there isn't! We have to clear things up about Hovea.'

'Get real, Laverton. Go play happy families with your city girl. You're wasting your time here. Whatever we might have had is over.'

'What do you mean, over? We haven't even begun!'

The panic surged upward from her belly and almost engulfed Rosy. What did he mean we haven't even begun? She didn't want anything from Benedict, ever. She made a sudden dash for the steps. She was at the top and desperately trying to get the key in the lock before Benedict realized what she was doing. He shot up the steps behind her, clamping his hand over her fumbling cold fingers. 'This is madness. Listen to me, Rosy.'

'Let go!'

Benedict grabbed Rosy's shoulders and hauled her around to face him. 'I will when you stop running. Hovea was lying tonight.'

'Oh yeah? I believe you!' Her sarcasm was loud and scathing.

Benedict made an agonized groan under his breath and dropped his hands. 'I don't understand you, Rosy. Why won't you give me a chance?'

'Because you're a man. Because men

lie. I know. It's happened to me before and I'm not being played for a fool again!' Rosy spat at him.

'I'm not like your ex-husband,' Benedict almost shouted back. 'I wouldn't lie to you Rosy. Give me a chance to prove myself to you. Give us a chance!'

'No!' She held her hands over her ears to block him out.

'Rosy, please!'

'Go away. I'm tired and I want to go to bed. And,' she gave Benedict a quelling look. 'I don't want to see you again.'

This time Benedict didn't stop Rosy from unlocking the door. She wrenched it open, slipped through, and banged it shut behind her. She leaned against it, her heart raced and the blood pumped loudly in her temples. Under the churning anger was a bleak sense of loss. In the few short days she'd known Benedict, she'd come to respect the man. Cared for him, against her better judgment. She'd told herself not to get involved, but she'd done just that and the searing pain in her heart made her feel absolutely desolate.

At the sound of the Jaguar roaring throatily away, Rosy's shoulders slumped in despair. He'd gone. She'd never see him again. Depression settled around her like the dark night. Her head throbbed and her neck was stiff and sore from awkwardly dozing in the taxi. She felt plain defeated. Slowly she straightened and tiptoed through the still house, until she remembered the boys were at Janice's. There was no need to be quiet. The realization depressed her further.

In the bathroom, she stared long and hard at her reflection in the basin mirror. Large, brown reproachful eyes stared back. What was it about her that attracted the wrong type of man? It wasn't as if she was a failure in other parts of her life. She was a good mum, a loyal friend, a good masseuse, and not a bad footy coach. She was just a lousy judge of men.

She glanced down at her dress. What

a joke. When Janice had persuaded her to wear it, she'd actually felt sexy. Now she felt about as an alluring as a stale cocktail sausage. She stripped off the scrap of red material, bundled it into a ball, and flung it into the laundry basket. What a disastrous evening. She turned on the hot water tap as far as it would go and, once the steam began fogging the bathroom, she stepped into the tiled recess and had a long, scalding shower.

After toweling herself dry, she pulled on her warmest, baggiest tracksuit and slid between the icy sheets of her bed. It seemed a vast and lonely wasteland, mocking her for the inadequacies that plagued her life. Would there ever be a man trustworthy enough for her to love and share her world? Somehow she doubted it. Her depression darkened until it almost suffocated her. A lone tear trickled from the corner of her eye and melted into the pillow. She sniffed and held the heels of her hands against her eyelids to prevent any more from escaping. She would not cry. Men weren't worth it. Benedict definitely wasn't worth it.

So why did she feel so wretched?

Once she had her tears under control, Rosy lay there as taut as a bowstring for several minutes, just listening. She couldn't remember the last time she'd been in the house on her own. The only noises were from the animals: the squeaking rat's wheel, the feather-ruffling of the parrot, and the snores of the old dog who hadn't even bothered to welcome her when she'd returned.

For hours, Rosy twisted and turned while sleep evaded her. She thumped and pummeled her pillows, fluffed up her quilt, and stared sightlessly into the darkness, but sleep refused to play ball. She toyed with the idea of going for a run, but it was cold and dark, and anyway, physically she felt like the living dead. But her brain whirred at full velocity, replaying the events of the evening and especially Benedict's words: we haven't even begun. They had become an insidious mantra in her brain, mocking her. Surely Benedict could see they were doomed from the start. There was no reason to continue. No future. Any relationship they had would only end in tears.

And they would probably be all hers.

★ ★ ★

'So, did you have a great night?' asked Janice the next morning when she brought the boys home.

Rosy buried her face into the sweet smelling neck of Joshua and inhaled his scent before returning a muffled answer.

'What was that?' Janice asked, dumping the boys' bags on the floor. 'I didn't quite catch what you said.'

Rosy reluctantly gave Joshua one more cuddle before he squirmed away to join Matt and Henry the dog outside. She faced her friend. 'I said it was informative.'

'So does that translate as great?'

'Nope.'

Janice slumped. 'Ah rats, and after all that planning.'

'You knew we were going to Perth?' Janice nodded. 'And the helicopter?' She nodded again. 'You didn't think to tell me?'

'I thought it'd be exciting!'

'That's what Laverton said. It wasn't. It was a complete failure.'

'Oh Rosy, what a shame.'

'Actually, no, it wasn't. It clarified things for me. You see, Jan, I was in danger of making an utter fool of myself over Benedict Laverton and, thankfully because of last night, I've been saved that humiliation.'

'The evening couldn't have been that bad?'

'Worse! But it made me see that Benedict Laverton's world and mine wouldn't mix. It would've been stupid to try.'

'Oh, come on, Rosy, he's not an alien. He's a decent bloke who happens to have a load of money. I think you're making too much out of your differences. You want the relationship to fail. You're too chicken to give it a proper go.'

Rosy gave Jan a level look. 'I know what I'm talking about. It wouldn't have worked out between us.'

'I don't like the sound of past tense. You are going to be seeing him again, aren't you? You aren't going to call it quits after one duff night?'

'There was nothing to quit. We hadn't even begun.'

'But you were getting on famously. You're made for each other. Goodness, the air just about crackles when you're in the same room. You can't not see him again. This man could be the love of your life.'

'He isn't. And I won't be seeing him again!'

'You sound very sure about that.'

'I am. No doubt about it.'

'And Benedict agrees with you?'

'Of course.' Hopefully, if he's reasonable.

'Well, I find that hard to believe. I'm sure he's smitten. He never takes his eyes off you when you're together and when he talks about you there's a special warmth in his voice. I'll be very surprised if he gives up without a fight. He gives me the impression he's a man who wouldn't toss in the towel if he wants something. Or someone.'

'I'm not seeing him again, Jan.'

'Okay, okay. I was only offering my opinion. You were there, you know best. Though I still think you're being chicken!'

There was a short, sharp knock on the back door and both women turned towards it. Benedict walked in dressed in black tracksuit pants, blue sports shirt, black jumper, and joggers. Apart from his tired eyes, he looked great. And lethal. As if he meant business. As if he was intent on an important quest. Rosy hoped against hope she wasn't the quest.

'No doubt, eh?' Janice raised her brows at Rosy.

'Shut up,' said Rosy as her heart pounded erratically in her chest. She hadn't expected

256

to see him again. Well, maybe she had. Like Janice, she believed Benedict wouldn't give up without a good fight. But she hadn't expected to see him quite so soon. Wasn't he going to allow her any breathing space?

'What are you doing here?' she said, her voice cold and hostile, masking her inner confusion.

'Footy practice. Hi, Janice. Thanks for babysitting last night.' His voice was tight and controlled. Rosy's heart beat faster.

'You're welcome. Anytime. Sorry it wasn't a better night,' said Janice.

'Never mind. Next time it will be.'

'So there will be a next time,' Janice said conversationally, giving Rosy a smug I-told-you-so look.

'There will be no next time,' said Rosy through gritted teeth.

'There is no baby,' said Benedict.

'Baby?' Janice queried. 'What baby? Am I missing something here?'

'It's not important,' said Rosy.

'It was last night,' said Benedict. 'So

important you ran out on me again. It's becoming a habit, Rosy, and I don't like it.' He slammed his hands on his hips and glared at her. Rosy shivered inside, but she wasn't going to be bullied. She would keep on running! It was much safer than staying anywhere near Benedict.

'Well, it's one you won't have to worry about again, will you,' she said with bravado.

'You promise not to do it again? That's reassuring.' There was more than a hint of sarcasm in his voice.

'The only thing I'm promising you, Laverton, is not to see you again. I thought I made that plain last night?' It was her turn for hands on hips and a pugnacious look.

'You're being totally unreasonable, Rosy.'

'I've a right to be. There's a baby in the equation here.'

'As far as I know, Hovea is not pregnant.'

'But you've slept with her.' It was a statement, not a question.

Benedict scowled even more, streaks of angry red slashing his cheekbones. 'No!' he barked. 'Not once.'

'You're good, Laverton, I'll give you that. You almost sound convincing.' She did a slow handclap. 'You could win an Oscar for your performance.'

'For God's sake, Rosy, I'm telling you the truth!'

'So you say. But you're an attractive man, she's an attractive woman, and she says she's having your baby. What am I supposed to think?'

'I categorically deny sleeping with Hovea. The whole idea fills me with repugnance.'

'Why? She's gorgeous.'

'I've never fancied her like that. We've never been more than good friends.'

Rosy chewed her bottom lip. She was very confused. 'I've had enough of all this. I don't care about your sex life, Laverton.'

She lied. She cared a great deal.

'It has nothing to do with me.'

She lied. It had everything to do with

her, because it crucified her heart.

'I'm off to coach the boys. And you,' she jabbed Benedict in the chest, 'do not need to come. We can cope perfectly well without you.'

Once she got him out of her system and locked his memory away with all her other heartbreaks. Goodness, when would she ever learn!

She stalked out the room, snapping the fly screen door shut. Janice gave Benedict a bemused look. 'Okay,' she said. 'Let's start at the beginning. Who's Hovea and where does this baby come into it?'

'It's a long story,' said Benedict, shaking his head. He filled in Janice with the pertinent facts. 'So it's all a big misunderstanding, but Rosy doesn't seem to want to straighten things out. She'd rather block me out of her life than work things through. It's as if she's scared of me. I really don't know how to crack it with her and it's driving me nuts.'

'Rosy isn't that complicated,' said Janice. 'She's been dumped on by men and she has no intention of getting hurt again. She's being cautious, that's all. She has to be. You'll have to be patient and give her time to get used to you, to trust you. Of course, there is one way to win some important brownie points with her.'

'How?'

'Through her boys.'

'Such as?'

'Buy them footy shirts.'

'Footy shirts? That sounds too easy.'

'For the whole team.'

'Ah.'

'And then, of course, you could volunteer for the fun run. That would give her plenty of warm, fuzzy feelings. She loves it when her friends pitch in and suffer for charity. She was thrilled when I entered it last year and not so thrilled when she heard I'd be away on holiday for this one. But personally, I can't see any fun in a run. It almost killed me doing the distance, so I was fully prepared with an excuse to skip the run this time round.'

'How long is this fun run?' Benedict

asked suspiciously.

'It's ten kilometers. Piece of cake for someone in your condition.'

'Ten? I can barely manage one.'

'Better get into training then.' Janice laughed and patted his arm. 'Better you than me, but good luck all the same.'

Benedict went slowly out of the door. Okay, the shirts sounded simple enough. He'd get his secretary on that. But the run? Hmm, that would take a lot more effort. He could set up a treadmill in his office, he could put in a mobile gym too, and he could up the number of lengths he swam daily in his pool. Benedict felt the stirrings of a challenge. There was a long slog ahead of him, but he was prepared to do whatever was needed to win Rosy. He'd show her he meant business.

Suddenly, he felt a lot more confident about winning Rosy Scott's heart.

He gave Rosy an easy grin as he joined her and the team in the backyard and began to limber up, ignoring her ferocious glare.

'I'm here to stay, so get used to it, Coach,' he said.

'You're surplus equipment.'

'You need me.'

'Never!' Though Rosy wasn't quite clear about personally or for the team. And she wasn't going to ask for clarification. That would be much too dangerous. 'I'll let Henry off the chain,' she threatened.

'That's playing dirty.'

'You don't deserve any better.'

'If he trips me up, I'll demand another massage.'

'Dream on, Laverton.' In spite of herself, Rosy felt fire course through her at the idea of a massage. *Oil and flesh, his flesh, under her hands . . .*

'Everyone needs their dreams. Now, come on, Coach, let's play some footy. Unless, of course, you want to spar all day?'

Rosy shivered. She hated herself for wanting to do just that. She enjoyed their verbal warfare. She enjoyed everything about him.

Except his womanizing.

While Rosy loved the special way he made her feel, she was a one-man woman and, in return, she wanted to be loved by a one-woman man. The frozen lump of depression deep inside suddenly doubled in size. She felt suffocated. She had to get away from him.

'I can't do this,' she muttered. 'You coach the boys. I'm going for a run.'

Benedict pursed his lips. 'Running away again, Rosy?' he said.

'You got a problem with that, Laverton? Or can't you handle this mob of boys on your own?'

'I can handle the boys just fine. It's you I'm having the difficulty with.'

'My heart bleeds.'

'So does mine,' he returned so quietly Rosy thought she'd misheard him. Except, he looked as though he meant it. Her heart fluttered as if a thousand birds were caged within it. She resolutely turned away.

'Don't work the boys too hard,' she shot at him as she began to jog towards the back gate. 'And don't be here when I get back.'

Benedict watched her lithe form disappear from view, her ponytail swinging from side to side, and wished he could follow. He was sure, given the time, she would believe him about Hovea. If only she would stand still long enough for him to convince her of his innocence.

With a sigh, he turned to the boys who were already tossing the ball to each other. 'Come on, lads,' he said. We've some work to do.'

12

Late Friday night the doorbell jangled. Rosy's heart did a massive flip-flop in her chest and then began to pound as fast as a herd of stampeding water buffalo. Each time, Rosy experienced a rush of acute, suffocating hope it might be Benedict. She hadn't heard from him since she'd run out on him during Saturday's training session. Not a peep. She kept telling herself that was exactly how she wanted it. But a traitorous part of her missed him dreadfully. Everything was gray and dismal without him. No teasing, no casual affection, and no underlying throb of sexual promise. She felt so wimpy wanting to hear from him. It was like being a lovesick teenager all over again.

'Answer the door! Answer the door!' said Matthew's pink and gray parrot. It shuffled up and down its perch, bobbing its head, as the bell rang again.

'Okay, Bert, give me a break,' said Rosy, sneaking a quick peek in the hallway mirror to make sure her hair wasn't too messy and her face clean. Just in case.

She opened the door. Her smile froze. 'Hovea!' Not Benedict. Disappointment washed through her, quickly followed by resentment. What was she doing here?

'Hi, Rosy.' The woman looked out of place and awkward. 'May I come in?'

'If you're looking for Benedict, he's not here,' Rosy said shortly. She did not want this woman, the cause of her misery, in her home.

'Actually, I wanted to see you.'

'Oh? Why?'

'I'd rather not discuss it on your doorstep. It's, er, a delicate matter.'

'I suppose, in that case, you'd better come in,' said Rosy grudgingly. She led Hovea into the kitchen, feeling conscious of her old blue jeans and washed out shirt. The thick woolly purple socks didn't lessen her feeling of inferiority either. She really must invest in some new clothes a pair of decent slippers.

Hovea, of course, was immaculate. She wore a black tailored suit and ivory silk blouse. Even after her three-hour car journey, the suit was crisp and smart, her hair sleek and smooth, her make-up perfect.

'Can I get you anything? Tea? Coffee?'

'Black coffee, thanks. No sugar.'

While Rosy made it, she cast surreptitious glances at Hovea. She wondered what she wanted. Surely there was nothing they had to say to each other. But whatever it was about, Hovea was extremely nervous and that, in turn, made Rosy wary. 'Here you go,' said Rosy, placing two chunky sky-blue pottery mugs on the scarred Formica table and invited Hovea to sit down opposite her.

'I want you to talk to Benedict,' Hovea said without preamble.

Surprised, Rosy stared at her in

silence for several seconds. 'Why?'

'Because he won't make a commitment about the baby.' Hovea sounded almost petulant. 'And I think that's your fault.'

Rosy lowered her eyes, hoping to hide her distress from Hovea. She blew at the steam as it curled from her full mug of coffee. 'Don't blame me for Benedict's infidelity!' she said sharply.

See, he was like Steve and Rick! She had been right to cut him out of her life, however much she missed him.

'But everything was all right until he met you. You've changed him,' accused Hovea.

'I'm not having an affair with him, Hovea. I'm not responsible for any of Benedict's actions.'

'But you are! He's totally besotted with you. It's so unlike Benedict to be infatuated with a woman. But you have bewitched him. He spends less time at the office and all his weekends down here with you.' Hovea twined her fingers in agitation. 'Do you mind if I smoke?' she said.

'Yes, I do, actually, and you shouldn't be smoking if you're pregnant. You'll damage the baby.'

'There is no baby,' said Hovea, two bright spots of red, like beacons, suddenly appeared in the pale expanse of her cheeks.

'What?' Rosy experienced a rush of blood to her head. Had she heard right?

'There is no baby.' The beacons flared brighter.

Rosy's heart contracted sharply. Had Benedict been telling the truth after all? Lord, why had she not believed him? Had she thrown away a real chance of happiness?

'But you said the other evening you were pregnant!' And ruined what could have been a fantastic night.

'No, what I said was Benedict and I were going to have a baby,' said Hovea defensively.

'But that's the same thing!'

'No, it isn't. And now he won't even discuss it. If you told him it was okay, we can carry on and have one.'

'What do you mean?' Rosy was confused.

'It won't have any bearing on your relationship. You and Benedict can have your affair. I won't interfere. I'm not the clingy sort.'

'Hold it right there, Hovea! Start at the beginning. You've completely lost me,' said Rosy. If she'd been a smoker she would have grabbed one of Hovea's cigarettes to calm down. None of this made sense. She rose from her chair and paced up and down the bright kitchen, her arms folded tightly in front of her chest.

Hovea squeezed her eyes shut and rubbed her temples with her fingertips. It was obvious she was under a lot of strain. Rosy could empathize! She was feeling pretty strained too. 'Have you anything stronger?' Hovea asked, pushing away her untouched coffee.

Rosy did a rapid think. 'Only sherry.' She left out the 'cooking' part. In this instance, she didn't think it mattered to

Hovea. She needed a fix of something strong. Rosy put two glasses on the table and poured each of them a generous amount of the cheap sherry. 'Cheers,' she said, clinking Hovea's glass. 'Now explain what's going on.'

'It's very simple and straightforward. I'm thirty-six and single. I have a brilliant, fulfilling career, plenty of money in the bank, an impressive investment portfolio, and a luxury apartment. All I want now is my own child to complete the picture.' She stopped and took a sip of sherry. She grimaced slightly and gave Rosy a slightly reproachful look. 'This is awful stuff,' she said.

Rosy shrugged. 'It's all I have. Sorry.'

'I suppose it doesn't matter.' Hovea took another tentative sip, shuddered, and said, 'I've known Benedict for years. He's a good friend and I thought he'd be an ideal person to father the baby.'

'And he doesn't?'

Hovea laughed without mirth. It

sounded brittle and strained. 'He was shocked, I think, by my suggestion. But I'm sure if you hadn't been on the scene, he would have agreed to it. It makes sense. We're both single, wealthy, and have a great deal of respect for each other. Our baby would have had all the trappings. All the advantages. But then you came along and spoiled it all.'

'I think you overrate my role in this.'

'He would have gone along with it!' Hovea sounded almost fierce. 'Men always balk at personal commitment, but I would have persuaded him in the end. Goodness, all I wanted was his genetics, not his head on a platter! It's no big deal.'

It was to Rosy. She found Hovea's attitude startling. 'So you don't love him?' she said. In spite of herself, she felt a great wave of relief when Hovea answered.

'Love him? No! Well, not like that.'

'Then why pick Benedict to father your child?'

'I respect him. I know a lot of men,

Rosy, but Benedict is probably the most dependable and reliable man of my acquaintance. He's your typical Mr. Good Guy. He's always there for you if you get in a fix. I trust him. He's kind and generous. But then you know all this. You've spent time with him.'

Rosy was silent. I didn't believe him, she thought in despair. I didn't trust him. His generosity and charm I tainted with my suspicions. I misjudged him and measured him against others less worthy. Lord, what have I lost through my own stupid prejudice? Rosy slung back her sherry and topped off both their glasses. She could feel Hovea's intense gaze on her.

'You will talk to him?' Hovea finally broke the silence. There was a pleading urgency in her tone.

'No.' Rosy shook her head. 'This is between the two of you. I'm sorry, Hovea, but I'm old fashioned. I believe in love and marriage. My own marriage didn't work out, but that doesn't mean I don't think that's the right order of things — love, marriage, and then children. But your situation has nothing to do with me. Anyway, I doubt if I'll be seeing Benedict again. We didn't part on good terms. But even if I did, I still wouldn't interfere.'

Hovea covered her face with her hands and began to cry with big gulping sobs, rocking backwards and forwards, smudging her mascara and lipstick. 'But I want a baby!' she cried. 'I want a baby!'

Though Rosy was embarrassed by the sudden storm of weeping, she was also profoundly moved by Hovea's despair. At least Rosy had her precious boys. Whatever mess the rest of her life was in, she had their unstinting, unquestioning love. Nobody could take that away from her. She wrapped her arms around Hovea's shaking body and gave thanks for her own circumstances. She didn't envy Hovea her high-flying lifestyle one iota. She didn't know what to say to the distraught woman, but she held her tightly in her arms, made soothing noises, and comforted her as if Hovea was one of her children.

'Sorry,' Hovea said once her crying had come to an end.

'Don't be.' Rosy gave her one last hard hug and then poured out another glass of sherry. 'We all have our tough times. No one is immune.'

Hovea blinked a couple of times and blew her nose. Her smooth pale cheeks were mottled and mascara streaked, her blue eyes red and swollen. 'I came here to intimidate you,' she said. 'I was so desperate and angry and believed you were the cause.'

'Don't worry about it. We all make mistakes.' Like I misjudged Benedict, thought Rosy.

Hovea sighed. 'You're very kind and understanding. I can see why Benedict's so infatuated.'

Rosy gave a hollow laugh. 'You've got that wrong too. Our relationship, such as it was, bordered on non-existent. I don't think that's going to change in a hurry. So you see, we've both lucked out where Benedict is concerned.'

'Damn!' said Hovea and tossed back her sherry.

'I'll drink to that.' Rosy copied the action. They both winced as the rough alcohol hit the back of their throats. Their eyes met. They both grinned sheepishly and then they began to laugh.

'The sherry does taste better the more you drink,' Rosy gasped through the giggles.

'I do hope so,' Hovea answered, rubbing her streaming eyes on the back of her hand. 'But let's drink to it, all the same.' The chinked glasses and took another gulp.

'Here's to men, God bless them,' said Rosy.

'And women,' said Hovea. They saluted each other and drank some more.

'And babies,' added Hovea, as an afterthought.

Somewhere, between toasting life and any other suitable topic, Rosy and

Hovea moved into the sitting room. They sat on the floor, swapping stories and experiences. By the time the sherry bottle was empty, the women were comfortably mellow and had formed a firm friendship.

When the doorbell suddenly pealed, Rosy had no idea of the time except it was very, very late. Too late for any of her friends to be calling. So she ignored it.

'Aren't you gonna get that?' hiccupped Hovea.

'Nope, can't be bothered. It's probably just some kids mucking about.'

'What if it's a friend?'

'Too late. They'll go away in a minute.'

The bell rang again. 'Ssh,' said Rosy in a loud stage whisper. 'Or you'll wake the kids.'

Hovea giggled. 'I don't think they heard,' she said as the bell was followed by a knock. They then heard the front door open. They exchanged a startled glance.

'Rosy?' said a deep, husky voice that penetrated Rosy's psyche and made her wonder if she'd overdone the sherry drinking. It sounded like Benedict, but surely not?

'Can I come in?' He popped his head around the sitting room door and smiled one of his bone-melting smiles at Rosy. It slipped a bit when he saw Hovea sitting on the floor next to her and then he frowned.

Both women stared at him in mute surprise and then back to each other. Then they began to laugh. 'We're not hallucinating, are we?' said Rosy, whose heart had gone straight into its high-speed flip-flopping routine at the sight of him.

'Don't think so,' said Hovea. 'Looks awfully like Benedict to me.' She crooked her finger and gave a little wave in his direction. His smile slipped completely. The frown got worse.

Rosy blinked at him. He held a huge bunch of red roses in one hand and had his other arm around a huge cardboard box. She blinked again to make sure.

279

Yep, she wasn't hallucinating. 'Hello, Benedict.' She hoped she didn't sound too pathetically breathless, though it didn't stop her from feeling it. His sheer magnetism filled her small sitting room and lapped around her. Seeing him again made her feel light-headed. 'Come in and join us.'

'You've been drinking!' He sounded outraged and Rosy couldn't help but giggle at his scandalized tone.

'You can have one too, if there's any left,' said Hovea, trying to peer down the neck of the bottle.

'If it's the cooking sherry, no thanks. What are you doing here, Hovea? You're a long way from home.' He sounded very suspicious, as if she was there to hound him about the baby.

'Don't worry, darling,' Hovea said with a slightly slurred laugh. 'I haven't come to force you into this baby-thing. Not unless you want to be persuaded?'

'No!'

Hovea sighed, regret shimmering in her eyes. 'Thought as much. It wasn't a very sound idea anyway — born out of desperation. Sorry.'

Benedict looked awkward, but relieved, like a man on death row who's had his sentence reprieved. He glanced at the flowers and the box. Abruptly he handed the roses to Rosy and then dumped the box in the hall. When he re-entered the room, Rosy was fondling one of the rich red, velvety petals.

'These for me?' she asked huskily.

'Yeah.' He fidgeted from one foot to the other and rammed his fists into his pinstriped trousers pockets, as if he was embarrassed about giving flowers.

'It's been years since anyone gave me flowers.' She felt ridiculously warm and fuzzy. She wasn't sure if it was because Benedict was there, because she'd been given roses, or because she'd drunk too much of the cooking sherry. Whatever the reason, she didn't care. She felt better than she had all week.

'If you're going to get all mushy, I'm going home,' said Hovea trying to get to her feet.

'You can't drive in your condition,' said Benedict putting out a hand to steady her. 'I'll take you back to Martha's. You can stay the night there. She won't mind.'

'I think I'll take you up on that offer. Goodness, what was that stuff?' she said, attempting to read the empty bottle's label.

'You don't want to know!' said Benedict with feeling.

As Hovea wove her way through the door, Benedict turned to Rosy. He took two measured steps so he stood over her. He hunkered down and reached out, tipping up her chin so he could look into her dreamy eyes. He then very, very slowly leaned toward her until his lips were millimeters away. 'I'll be back soon, if that's okay with you?'

Rosy gave him a slow, sexy smile. 'I'll be waiting,' she said.

Benedict breathed in her scent that mingled with the heavy seductive perfume of the roses. His gut clenched in heated need for her. His heart began to hammer a million beats a second. He closed the distance between them so their lips fused as one. With tantalizing slowness, he moved his mouth over her sherry-sweet lips. It was sheer heaven, until a nervous cough and giggle broke the spell.

'Sorry,' said Hovea. 'But I couldn't find the car.'

Benedict sighed, resting his forehead against Rosy's. 'I'll be as quick as I can.'

★   ★   ★

Later, Benedict let himself back into Rosy's house. Apart from the rhythmic squeak of the rat's exercise wheel, the place was silent. A lamp illuminated the hall and another the lounge. The floorboards creaked as he stealthily crept through the rooms, trying to find Rosy. The bedroom was empty. He frowned and tiptoed back into the lounge. There, curled up on the sofa, was Rosy. Her hair was loose and tousled about her face, her lips were

283

slightly open, eyes closed. She was out for the count.

Benedict let out a long sigh. That cooking sherry was lethal. It should carry a government health warning. Hovea had fallen asleep as soon as he'd started the car and it had been very awkward trying to get her into his mother's spare bedroom and settling her down for the night. She'd wound her arms around his neck and whispered outrageous things to him. He hoped she wouldn't remember anything about it in the morning, because if she did it would embarrass the both of them. It had all taken much longer than he'd anticipated and it had only been thanks to his highly amused mother that he'd been able to escape at all.

He now gazed down at Rosy. His heart squeezed tight and tenderness flowed through him. He felt an overwhelming sense of homecoming. He brushed his fingertips across her cheek. The skin was dewy-soft and silken. He moved to the shadowed hollow of her throat and held his fingers lightly there, absorbing her throbbing pulse. His body tightened. Benedict suddenly wanted her with an intense surge of desire, but paradoxically he also wanted to gather her to him and hold her against his pounding heart and protect her.

Forever.

Now where the hell did that little thought pop from? Benedict shook his head, trying to clear his thoughts. When had Rosy become so important to him? It was ridiculous. He'd known her for such a short time, barely two weeks, and yet she'd burrowed into his heart and into his very soul. Not seeing her for the past week had been purgatory. But it wasn't just about the past seven days, it was as if he'd missed her all his life.

For years, he'd convinced himself he didn't need anyone special. He'd always been an island, not wanting or seeking to change his isolation. Rosy had changed all that with her big-hearted, energetic attitude to life. He was suddenly very conscious of what he'd been missing with his self-imposed exile and now he wanted to be part of Rosy's charmed circle, be part of her destiny. He no longer wanted to be on the outside.

He'd come home.

Now all he had to do was convince Rosy. It wouldn't be easy, thanks to her deeply ingrained suspicion of men. And, of course, her boys. Yep, they were a problem, sort of. But nothing he couldn't handle. He had to admit, Josh was an endearing urchin and easy to love. But Matthew? Ah, Matthew. He understood the boy all too well. He'd been there too. It would take time to gain his confidence. In fact, it would all take time, especially persuading Rosy into taking a gamble on their relationship and forging a commitment.

But first, he had to get her to bed. He hefted her into his arms and carried her to the bedroom. He undid her jeans and briefly considered taking them off so she'd be more comfortable. But he didn't think he could stand the strain of not kissing her, not touching her, and . . .

Benedict's composure was already stretched to the max after holding her pliable body in his arms and having the soft, clean scent of lemon soap and shampoo tantalize his senses. He resolutely covered her over with the quilt and walked away.

He found a rug and banked up the cushions on one end of the sofa. As a makeshift bed, it was a good two-foot too short, but it would have to do. The parrot ruffled its feathers and dinged its bell a couple of times.

'Pretty boy, pretty boy,' it said as Benedict shucked his trousers.

'Very funny, now go to sleep,' muttered Benedict, snapping off the lamp.

'Go to sleep,' said the bird, smacking the bell again. It repeated its refrain at lest twenty more times. Benedict considered whether or not to throw a shoe at it, but decided he'd wake up the household and the amount of satisfaction there'd be in silencing the bird wouldn't be worth it. Instead, he trooped to the kitchen, gathered a handful of tea towels, and tossed them over the birdcage.

He settled back down, thumped the cushions into a more comfortable shape, and shut his eyes. Then the rat wheel began squeaking. Squeak, squeak, squeak. Benedict shoved a cushion over his head. It took him a long time to fall asleep.

★ ★ ★

'Mum! Mum!' The urgent whisper brought Rosy from a deep, refreshing sleep. She cranked open an eye. Matthew was two inches away from her face.

'Hi, sweetie.' She held open the quilt for him to crawl into bed for a cuddle. The boy shook his head, declining the invitation.

'Mum, Zorro's escaped,' he said.

The rat? 'Oh, Lord. Where's the cat?'

'He's in the lounge trying to catch him.'

Oh, Lord!

'But, Mum?'

'Yes?'

'Mr. Laverton's in there too. Asleep.'

OH, LORD!

Rosy snapped into a sitting position. She rapidly pushed her hair out from her eyes, looping it haphazardly behind her ears. He came back! He stayed! She glanced down at herself. Yesterday's yellow T-shirt and blue jeans were undone! Grief, he must have put her to bed. That's right, she remembered now, she was sitting on the couch, waiting for him to come back, feeling all warm and fuzzy and . . .

'Come on, Mum, hurry up. Zorro's under the sofa and Mr. Laverton's on top.'

'Okay, okay, I'm coming. Grab the cat and throw him outside — but, Matt, do it quietly! We mustn't wake Mr. Laverton.' Not until she'd showered, changed, and put on a little lippy! 'I've already tried. Moondyke scratched me.' Matthew showed her his arm. Rosy gave it a quick kiss as Matt started to pull her toward the lounge.

'Let's go then,' said Rosy, sacrificing her hair and trying to re-snap her jeans. At the sofa she stopped. Benedict looked the picture of innocence with his tousled black hair and closed, heavily fringed lids that hid those all too perceptive gray eyes. She almost caressed his sleep flushed-cheek, but didn't, not with Matt hopping from one foot to the other and loudly whispering about Moondyke.

Rosy redirected her attention to the cat. Moondyke's yellow eyes were fixed on a spot under the sofa. 'Up you come, Moonie,' whispered Rosy, whisking up the cat and taking him, thrashing claws and tail, to the door. She tossed him out and closed the door quickly. She then hunkered down by the sofa and held up a corner of Benedict's blanket.

'Can't see him,' she mouthed to Matt.

Matt lay flat on his stomach and shone his torch. He nodded his head and pointed to where the rat was. They spent the next few moments trying to flush the rat out and into Matt's butterfly net. Matt prodded him with stick. The rat flew out one edge of the sofa, rushed up its arm, and buried himself under Benedict's blanket. Matt and Rosy shared a horrified glance and then Rosy began to giggle. She tried to muffle it with her hands clamped to her mouth. Matt grinned too and then began rolling about on the floor, silently shaking with laughter.

The lounge door suddenly banged open. Josh, pajamas half-mast and a teddy clutched under his arm, stood sleepily staring at them. 'What y'doin'?' he said as Moondyke rushed past him. At that precise moment, the rat surfaced for a peek, the cat sprang, and the rat dived south under Benedict's chin. The cat followed. So did Matt and Rosy. And they all landed on Benedict.

'What the devil?' Benedict roared

from sleep to fully awake in a nanosecond. The cat spat. Matt gasped. Rosy drew in a sharp breath and then exploded into further giggles. The rat took advantage of the confusion and burrowed deeper under the blankets, shooting down Benedict's bare legs.

'Wah!' Benedict jackknifed upwards and flung off the blanket. Rosy got an eyeful of muscular, hairy thighs before she concentrated on grabbing the blanket and smothering the cat.

'Morning, Laverton,' said Rosy as she bundled the furious cat out of the room. She shut the door and turned back to the scene of mayhem. Benedict had sprung off the sofa and was madly pulling on his trousers. Shame, she liked the casual look. He began buttoning up his shirt. Double shame. It was nice to see his strong, deep chest in daylight.

Benedict dragged a hand through hair, peaked from a rough night of disturbed sleep. 'Good grief, woman, is that any way to start the day?'

'Has to begin somehow.' She grinned. 'Need a coffee to settle the nerves?'

He gave her a jaundiced look. 'How come you look so breezy after last night? I thought you'd be the walking dead today.'

'Good metabolic rate.'

'But that sherry was poison.'

'My sherry isn't that bad.'

'Believe me, it's worse. Remind me to buy you some decent stuff.'

'Mum, we haven't caught Zorro yet,' interrupted Matt, who was staring hard at Benedict, a closed expression on his face.

'If you're talking about the rat, he's still under my blanket,' said Benedict.

'Would you help catch him while I have a quick shower and organize breakfast?' said Rosy, who'd just caught sight of her reflection in the sitting room mirror and was horrified by her feral appearance. Now was not the time to frighten off Benedict with scary hair. 'Good,' she said, not waiting for a reply. 'See you in a sec.'

She had the quickest shower and shampoo on record. She blasted her hair with the hairdryer and pulled on her tracksuit. She might want to impress Benedict, but she still had footy. It was their first match today and the team would turn up soon at the oval. There wasn't time to dawdle. She slicked on a hint of lip-gloss, just to add luster to her lips, nothing too obvious because she didn't want Benedict to think she was doing it to impress him, even if she was. She then headed for the kitchen to make a pot of porridge.

From the sound of it, Benedict and Matthew were having trouble with the rat. If they didn't catch it soon, they would have to shut the room up and hope to find Zorro when they returned from the match. It wasn't the first time the rat had gone AWOL and Rosy fervently hoped it wouldn't be for long. The previous escape resulted in an expensive visit from the fridge repairman after Zorro chewed through vital wires making a nest in the motor.

'Come on, you guys, or we'll be late,' she called out a few minutes later, ladling steaming oatmeal into bowls. When she received no answer, Rosy went and listened at the sitting room door. 'You okay in there?'

'Don't open the door!' shouted Matthew. There was a scuffle and thud. 'Way to go!' he yelled. 'Mr. Laverton's got him.' There was a yelp. 'And Zorro just bit him!'

Matthew came out grinning with Zorro, whiskers twitching, in his hands. Benedict followed, sucking his finger. 'Hope that thing hasn't got rabies,' he muttered and then squinted at his finger. 'It's drawn blood!'

'Poor baby,' said Rosy. 'Let's put some antiseptic on it before you start foaming at the mouth. And you, Matt, better put the rat away and secure his cage. We don't want him becoming a snack for Moondyke while we're out.'

Matt left the room talking soothingly to the rat and Benedict held out his finger to Rosy. 'Kiss it better,' he said, holding her eyes with his, a slight smile hovered around his mouth.

Rosy experienced a rush of heat. Even her toes tingled. She was sure her cheeks were flagged with red and Benedict would see how much effect he had on her.

'Go on, kiss it better. I dare you.'

'I think you'd be safer with a tetanus shot.'

'Cruel lady.'

'But in the absence of one, I think I can just about manage a kiss.' Rosy took his hand in both of hers and drew it towards her curving lips. She took her time, drawing his hand closer and closer. Was it her imagination, or did Benedict tremble slightly? Was he as vulnerable to her and she was to him? Happy thought!

There were little footsteps in the hallway, so she swiftly dipped her head and kissed the wound with lip-smacking efficiency. 'There, all better.' She lifted laughing eyes to his and patted his cheek as Matt returned to the kitchen and viewed them with suspicion. 'Now, let's put a band-aid on it and get moving. We've an important date at the oval.'

'What?' Benedict's voice sounded a mite husky. It made Rosy's heart beat with a faster rhythm. What a shame she couldn't kiss him properly, but with Matt in the room she thought it wiser not to. The boy was already resentful of Benedict's presence and she didn't want to make things worse.

'Our team's first match of the season,' she told Benedict.

'A proper game? Are they up to it?'

'As they'll ever be this season. But it's only a friendly, just to get them into the idea of it all and then next season they'll play junior league.'

'In that case, now's an appropriate time to show you something.' Benedict disappeared from the room and came back in with the same big box Rosy vaguely remembered him carrying in the night before. He dumped it on the kitchen floor and opened up the flaps.

He drew out something red and shook it into shape. It was a sleeveless shirt similar to those worn by professional football players. Benedict tossed it over to Rosy and then took out another and threw it to Matthew. Rosy stood wide-eyed, holding out the shirt before hugging it to her chest.

'Shirts! They're beautiful,' she said.

'For you. For the boys.'

'For us? Oh, wow! But why?'

'A present for you and the team. Because I heard you needed them and I wanted to do something for the kids other than toss a ball around.'

'But these shirts must have cost a packet! I can't accept them.'

'For someone who blithely spent ten thousand dollars of my money without batting an eyelid, I think you can. For the team.'

'I did bat an eyelid! I had cold sweats bidding all that dosh.'

'I'm glad to hear it.'

'But it doesn't mean I can accept these shirts . . .'

'Rosy, please, for me?'

'But . . . '

'Mum, they're great,' said Matthew. He added shyly, 'We could wear them today.'

Rosy appealed to Benedict. 'But . . . '

'No buts, princess. Accept them with good grace and they'll give the boys a psychological morale boost for today's game.'

'What can I say?'

'Thank you, Benedict.'

'Thank you, Benedict.'

Benedict grinned at her. She grinned back. Matthew scuffed his foot. 'I'm hungry,' he said.

'Oh, Lord, let's get breakfast on the go or we'll lose by default!' said Rosy. When they'd all sat down, Rosy said, 'How did you know we needed shirts?'

'Jan told me.' Benedict poured honey over his oats and waited. He could tell she found accepting the shirts a hard thing to do. Why? What was the big deal? They were only a pile of shirts. Organizations were always asking for sponsorship of such things without turning a hair.

'Oh.' She squirmed in her seat, ate a couple of spoonfuls and then said, 'You know, Laverton, you don't have to buy your way into our life. Don't get me wrong, I am grateful for the shirts. They're terrific. But you don't have to do those sorts of things.'

'Let me. I can afford it.' Easily. 'Money isn't a big issue with me. I've always had enough to do what I wanted to do. And I wanted to buy those darn shirts.' He was beginning to wish he hadn't! This was turning into something bigger than Ben Hur.

'Well, it is an issue with me. We don't have much. I'm not used people just giving us things. Around here, people tend to do things to help each other, not shell out money.'

'I'm 'doing' too,' said Benedict, stung to defend himself.

'Helping coach is great. I can handle that.'

'I'm so glad!'

'Now you're in a snitch. I was only trying to say . . . '

'I know what you're getting at. I can't help being rich, Rosy. But if I can live with it, I'm sure you can too. I'm not just coaching; I've entered your precious fun run.'

'Really?' She went pink with pleased surprise.

Janice had been right. Rosy did like her friends involved with her charities. He felt a certain smugness that he'd done well. He'd gained her favor.

'Yes, really. So what've you got to say about that, Ms. Scott?'

'It's brilliant. I suppose Janice coerced you into that too?'

'I wasn't coerced into anything. She just happened to mention it. As you had on the odd occasion.'

'Did she tell you when it was?'

'No.'

'Next Saturday.'

'Oh.' Saturday! Holy Moly! There was barely any time to train. He'd have to seriously up his hours on the treadmill

301

and exercise bike, let alone weight machines. But he tried to appear nonchalant. He didn't want Rosy to think she had the upper hand.

Rosy grinned at him. 'And did she tell you that you had to wear a costume?' she said sweetly.

13

'That was fun,' said Rosy. She was sprawled on the sofa with her feet propped up on a couple of cushions and another couple behind her head. She'd showered, changed, and was feeling nicely mellow. The last of the kids were still playing ball in the garden. Their shouts and laughter mixed with Henry's excited, deep-throated barking.

'Which bit?' said Benedict who sat on the floor, his back resting against the sofa, just about parallel to Rosy's thigh. 'The trouncing, the dog fight, or the after-match barbecue?'

'All of it. And it wasn't a trouncing. The boys held their own extremely well, under the circumstances. Those other kids were a good two years older than our eldest player.'

'I love the way you're so protective.'

Benedict grinned at her. 'They were trounced fair and square. Those kids just looked bigger because they weren't rolling in the mud for the majority of the game. Your boys hit the dirt at every opportunity. They should go on stage for their spectacular falls.'

Rosy giggled. 'They do get rather carried away.'

'So does their coach. I think my ribs are broken.'

'They scored. I had to hug someone.'

'Honey, you can hug me anytime.'

'I'll remember that.' Rosy batted her eyelashes and him. 'As for the dog fight, you were very brave saving Henry like that, especially after last week's training fiasco. It's good to know you don't hold grudges.'

'Henry is a psychotic dog with a death wish. What on earth possessed him to attack the mastiff?'

'He's never liked him. It goes back a long way.'

'He's fought him before?'

'Yup.'

'Who broke them up?' Rosy didn't answer. 'Don't tell me, you did!'

'So?'

'Don't. You could get really hurt.'

'I haven't yet.'

Benedict leaned over her, his arm resting along her denim-covered thigh, his eyes fiercely intent. Rosy was suddenly breathless, wondering what he was going to do. Kiss her? Yes, please! The heat from his arm fused with her leg and she kept herself from moving closer. She didn't want him to think she was begging for his kisses, though she had to admit she almost was. The air had vibrated with sexual electricity all day. The suspense of whether or not he was going to make a move on her was killing her! If he didn't hurry up, she'd have to throw caution to the wind and take control of the situation. Once the boys were safely tucked in bed, of course.

'There's always a first time and those dogs weren't messing around. It's one thing to be bitten by a rat, quite another by a dog,' Benedict said quietly.

'I wasn't the one rat-attacked this morning.' Her chest constricted at his obvious concern for her. When was the last time anyone really cared if she'd got hurt or not? The feeling was surprisingly uncomfortable. It didn't rest well with her. She wasn't sure if she could cope with being wrapped in cotton-wool. She'd fought her own battles for such a long time.

'Rosy, promise me you'll be careful. You'd best leave Henry here than take him to the oval.'

'He'd howl the place down.' She shifted her leg away as she spoke and buried her nose in her mug of coffee to avoid his eyes.

'Let him.' Benedict grabbed her leg and pulled it back towards him. 'Don't pull away just because I express concern.'

He was too perceptive by half, thought Rosy. No wonder he was such a successful businessman if he could read other people's minds.

'I'm not used to it,' said Rosy. 'And I don't invite it. Take me as you find me, Laverton, or not at all.' She abruptly got to her feet. 'I'd better tell those kids to go home before it gets dark. There's a pile of wash to do from the barbecue.'

'I'll make a start on it,' said Benedict, rising to his feet too. His hand rested lightly on Rosy's shoulder. 'And I'll take you any way you want me to,' he said, dropping a kiss on the top of her head before turning away and heading towards the kitchen.

'That a promise?' Rosy slung her hands on her hips and gave him a saucy look, to make up for her flash of churlishness. She didn't want to spoil their fragile new relationship.

'You better believe it.' His smile was slightly crooked and Rosy felt another sliver of resentment melt away. He was so damn irresistible it was hard to feel annoyed with him for long. He'd only said it because he cared.

'I'll hold you to it.'

'I was banking on it.' He retraced his

steps and cupped Rosy's head in his hands. They were warm and firm, strong, and tender. A lump rose in her throat and annoying tears suddenly filled her eyes. She wasn't used to this nurture business. It terrified her. It made her feel too vulnerable. She was the one who did the caring and looking after around here. Being on the receiving end was scary. It took all her will power not to bat his hands away and shove her irritatingly vulnerable feelings into their box. She felt so exposed to his dark-eyed scrutiny, as if he could look into her very soul and find her wanting. Perhaps that's what Steve and Rick had felt, that she was wanting.

A teardrop escaped and trickled down her cheek. Benedict's thumb swept it away, followed by his lips on her damp cheekbone. He kissed her with exquisite care, as if she was a precious, fragile thing. It was a small kiss, no passion attached, but it hooked her anyway. His lips then traced a trail to her lips. That kiss lasted only a moment too. Dang, she wished they lasted longer. She wanted more! But Benedict pulled away. He gazed down at her with such heat it made her heart rocket at a hundred miles a second. Would he kiss her again? Please!

But, no. He turned and left the room. Rosy watched him depart, kicking herself for feeling so disappointed. She wrestled with that disappointment. Of course he couldn't kiss her more, not with a pack load of boys racing around in her backyard. But there would be later. She would make sure of it. A shiver of pure longing rippled through her from the top of her head to the tip of her stripy, woolly-socked toes.

First things first, though. Children had to be dispatched home, dishes done, and her own kids showered, pajama-ed and put to bed.

Then she would make sure of it!

★   ★   ★

Rosy flicked the dishcloth over the stainless steel draining board for the zillionth time. The kids were in bed, the house was straight — it was crunch time! She fiddled a bit more as Benedict sauntered into the kitchen and stood very still only a few feet away from her. His eyes were dark but not fathomless. She knew exactly what was going on in those dark silvery depths! Rosy swallowed hard and did the flicking cloth routine to fill the sudden pressure-taut silence. She saw Benedict's lips twitch into a half smile and then he moved toward her.

Rosy's mouth was immediately as dry as the Simpson Desert. Her body, on the other hand, was all liquid fire. The simmering heat it had been operating on ever since Benedict had kissed her on stage at the auction was now several degrees hotter, almost boiling.

She swallowed again and flicked the cloth. Benedict was now only millimeters away, the air between them a crackling force-field of want, of need.

Benedict didn't say anything. He didn't have to. He took the cloth from Rosy and threw it into the empty sink. Rosy nervously wiped her hands on her backside.

What next?

As if she didn't know!

As if she wasn't hanging out for it!

Benedict hooked a finger in her jeans' waistband and drew her towards him. He deftly unsnapped the button and slowly slid down the zipper. Then, as his fingers brushed against her cotton knickers, his mouth was on hers, seeking her, needing her. Rosy's body heat flared higher, causing complete internal meltdown.

This was what she'd feared during Benedict's first kiss.

This was what she'd craved since that wonderful first kiss.

And this was going to happen now.

His mouth on her lips and his hand in her jeans was driving her wild. The heat was building to a furnace. She thought she'd melt in a heap at any moment. Her legs had gone weak and rubbery from desire. Her heart was racing full pelt. She needed him, all of him. But not by the sink, not in a place the boys might find them! 'Not here!' she managed to gasp between hot slick kisses. 'Bedroom . . . '

He carried her, kissing her the whole time. It took an age. It took a moment. Time meant nothing as the roaring, rippling passion burned in them, through them.

Inside the bedroom, the door closed so as not to wake the boys, it took them an instant to shed their clothes and tumble onto the sheets. In seconds Benedict possessed her, making her his, making her full of him. She possessed him just as completely, sucking him into the wondrous heat of her womanhood. Their bodies moved as one, as if they'd rehearsed the love act a thousand times and more, until the ultimate climax when they shattered against each other in complete accord.

Rosy's eyelids were glued shut. She lay in the dark, the faint squeak, squeak of Zorro's wheel a familiar background sound. She tried to gather her thoughts. Impossible. She tried to move her leg, but the effort was too much. A deep, sweet lethargy overwhelmed her body and her mind. Rosy floated, immersed in a complete sense of well-being.

She'd always experienced this almost euphoric weightlessness after running a marathon.

And after sex.

In the past five years, she'd only ever run marathons. She'd been too busy running away from relationship commitments to have sex.

Rosy let her mind drift for a moment, savoring the marvelous euphoria. Then she frowned. She hadn't run a marathon in a while. And she was naked. That meant . . .

Tentatively, she moved her arm a little to the left. It hit warm flesh

— taut, firm, living flesh. Flesh that belonged to Benedict. A thrill of electricity zipped through her.

Yup, it must have been the sex then.

Rosy slid her finger down his warm arm and let the electricity continue to course through her, re-igniting parts of her body that, seconds ago, had been inert in the aftermath of loving. Her body began to tingle and glow. She slid her hand lower. Benedict stirred. All of him stirred. He gave a sleepy, husky chuckle, drew Rosy into his warmth and began to nuzzle her neck.

'This is soooo good,' he breathed into her ear, sending shock waves of desire rocking through her.

'Quit talking, Laverton, and show me some action.'

'Yes, ma'am.'

Sometime later, Rosy surfaced again. She was spooned into the heated curve of Benedict's body. Contentment washed through her. This was a bliss she'd missed for so long. She sighed and let her eyelids fall shut for all of a split second.

The boys!

'Hey, Laverton, wake up.' He mumbled something indistinct and tightened his arm about her waist. Rosy dug a sharp elbow in his side. 'Wake up!'

'Oof! What?'

'You've got to go.'

'Ssh, go to sleep. Unless of course you want more?'

Rosy felt his body begin to harden. Her own flared in response, but Rosy resolutely ignored it. She did the elbow thing again. 'Get up, now!'

'Give me a couple seconds.' He gave a sleep-husked, sexy laugh.

'I don't mean that! I want you to leave. Go home. Now!' Rosy sat up, clicked on the bedside light and ripped the quilt off Benedict. Glory, he was a beautiful sight to behold. What a temptation. She clenched her hands so she wouldn't reach out to touch him.

'I don't want the boys to know you stayed over,' she whispered.

'Are you kidding?' Benedict fumbled for his watch. 'It's three in the morning!'

'Go, shoo!' Rosy slid out of bed and pulled on the nearest thing. It was a T-shirt that didn't quite hide everything.

'God, you're gorgeous!' His voice was graveled with desire.

'Stop gawking and get your clothes on.'

Benedict groaned. 'You're serious about this?'

'Deadly.' She chucked his jeans over to him and began searching for his shirt.

'The boys are going to have to know sometime.'

'Know what? There's nothing to know.'

'Then why am I being kicked out if this is nothing?' Benedict stopped putting on his socks to give her a questioning look.

'This was sex. They don't need to know their mother has sex.'

Benedict felt he'd been hit in the solar plexus with a sledgehammer. 'It wasn't just sex, Rosy. We made love.' He saw panic flare in her expressive brown eyes, but he didn't back down. It was time she faced facts. 'We made love and sooner or later they are going to realize we love each other.'

'We do not!'

'Rosy, when did you last sleep with a man?'

'I'm not going dissect my sex life at this time of night.'

'I'd bet my last dollar it was with your husband.'

'So? What does that prove?'

'You don't sleep around.'

'Well, Einstein, thank you for working that out. You really needed a Mensa score to deduct that. Because as a frazzled single mother of two boisterous boys, the men are hardly queuing up. Women with children scare men off.'

'You underestimate your allure, Rosy. A lot of men in this town would have happily stepped into Steve's shoes, but I've been told you weren't interested.'

'Too right.'

'Why?'

'It's 3:00 a.m., so stop asking questions and get dressed, for heavens sake!'

'I will after you explain.' Benedict crossed his arms and waited.

Rosy huffed and began marching up and down the room. Benedict tried not to stare at the glimpse of pale buttock peeking out from under the hem of the T-shirt. However sexy it was, he needed answers.

'Because once you sleep with a man in this town, it pretty much means commitment. I don't want to commit to anyone. I like my life how it is, sans a man.'

The sledgehammer hit the spot again. Benedict pulled on his shirt and started doing up buttons, trying not to feel angry and hurt. He guessed she'd said that to protect herself because of her own anger and hurt. 'So, how do you work out that sleeping with me doesn't constitute a commitment?'

'You're different. You're from out-of-town. You don't expect anything from me but sex.' Rosy stopped pacing and angled her jaw pugnaciously. Benedict realized she was challenging him to say otherwise.

'Okay,' he said, lacing his joggers.

'What do you mean, okay?'

Benedict glanced at Rosy. Her puppy-soft eyes viewed him suspiciously. With good reason! He wasn't going to accept just sex from Rosy. But now wasn't the time to tell her he had chosen her for life — for better, for worse. Because it was 3:00 a.m. on a cold winter's morning and she was a woman on a mission to get him out of the house before her children awoke. There were some things that just had to be delayed a while. Anyway, he needed time to re-group. He should have realized that any progress with Rosy would be complicated. One step forward and three steps back.

'Just that,' he said mildly. 'Sex is good. I'm glad we understand each other.'

He nearly laughed out loud when Rosy's eyes narrowed to thin slits of distrust.

'Good night, sweetheart. See you

319

tomorrow,' he said. He gathered her resisting body into his arms and kissed her soundly. He didn't know if her toes curled, but his certainly did. He would have liked nothing better than to crawl back under the covers with her and make more passionate love. Rosy might call it sex, but Benedict knew better. It was love, all right.

Rosy was fooling herself to think this was only about sex. She would have slept with a man before now if sex was all she wanted. No, she'd made love with him because she cared, because she wanted *him*. Now all he had to do was prove it to her.

He wanted more from Rosy than clandestine nights between the sheets.

He wanted everything.

★   ★   ★

'Is this something to do with the male menopause?' Martha asked Benedict a few mornings later. She had arrived unexpectedly at his Perth office and

320

found him clad only in shorts and T-shirt, covered in sweat, and pedaling the four-minute-mile on his exercise bike.

'Just trying to keep fit,' he puffed.

'A bike, a treadmill, and a bench press should certainly do that! Isn't it a little over the top for the office? Your father never indulged in such things. He found a round of golf quite adequate.'

'I am not my father.'

'I never said you were. But why all this frantic activity? Your secretary said you had this multi gym installed last week and you've been working out between meetings ever since.'

'You shouldn't gossip with my secretary.'

Martha gave a roguish smile. 'I never gossip, I simply ask succinct questions.'

'Same thing in my opinion.'

'Oh, fiddle!' She waved her hand dismissively and returned to her original question. 'So why all this exercising? And why, for goodness sake, don't you do it at home?'

'I do.'

'Oh, dear. You really must get a life, Benedict.'

'I'm working on it.'

'I meant with other people. You should settle down and raise a family. It would be good for you and good for me. I'd love to have some grandkids.'

'As I said, I'm working on it. Now, in the absence of grandchildren, how about you sponsor me?'

'What for?' Martha wrinkled her forehead.

'Coolumbarup Hospital's charity fun run.'

Martha's brows shot skywards. 'You've entered that?'

'Yes.'

'For this year's race?'

'Yes.'

'No wonder you're training so hard! It's a long way, darling. Are you up to it?'

'Yes!' Benedict took his feet off the pedals. The pedals carried on spinning of their own accord while he stiffly climbed off the bike. He snatched up a towel from the back of a black swivel chair and mopped at the droplets of sweat on his skin. 'What's your problem? It's for a good cause.' He didn't add 'my future as well as charity'.

'It benefits the children's ward, I know. But how come you're involved? No, don't tell me. Rosy Scott roped you in for it!' Martha suddenly grinned, as if she approved of the idea.

'Actually, no. I volunteered,' said Benedict, nettled by his mother's sudden glee.

'Ah.' Martha's eyes twinkled. 'You do know it's costume?'

'Yes, and you don't have to laugh quite so loudly. I can dress up with the best of them.' Benedict stopped blotting his brow and glared at his mother. 'What's the big deal?'

'What are you going as?'

'I've no idea yet.'

'Leave it to me, darling. I'll have something ready for Saturday morning.'

'Now why do I have a horrible feeling I'm not going to like your choice?'

'You're far too suspicious. Trust me.'

'Never!'

'Darling, how cruel! I only want the best for you.'

'Don't fail me, then.'

'As if!'

★ ★ ★

The giant chicken shedding feathers on the start line caused a great deal of merriment. Benedict blew a virulent, mustard-yellow feather from his mouth and vowed never, ever to trust a woman again. Between Rosy, Martha, and Janice he was made to look a prize turkey.

Except he was a chicken.

'Mr. Laverton, your feathers keep tickling my nose.' Benedict looked down at Josh.

'Sorry, mate. I must be molting. I might even lay an egg in a minute.'

Josh giggled. 'Have you seen Mummy?'

'Yeah, she's pretty cool, eh?' Rosy

324

had shown up at the oval dressed as the Queen of Hearts. 'Which one's mine?' he'd grinned at her.

'That'd be right, they're all made of paper,' Rosy had shot back before jogging off to check-in some latecomers to the fun run.

Benedict had shaken his head. She had a lot of healing to do. But he was a patient man. He would burrow under her reserve and show her, prove to her, he was worth the gamble.

The night before, after an explosive coming together and she'd lain satiated in his arms, he could almost feel her weaken and lay bare her soul. But Rosy had been on her own a long time and, in the wee small hours, he'd once again been booted from the cocooned warmth of her bed and into the nippy night.

'So, Drumsticks, are you feeling fit?' Rosy bounded up from a group of pirates and patted his tail feathers. She looked disgustingly healthy. Unlike Benedict, who suffered from his fractured night of lovemaking and bed-hopping.

'Not as fit as you. You appear to be thriving. I wonder why?'

Rosy gave a low chuckle. 'It's amazing how these night-time workouts limber one up!'

'Fine for those who stay snuggled in bed, while some of us have to brave the cold midnight air and drive along treacherous twisty and misty roads, dodging kangaroos and trying to keep awake long enough to get home.'

'If you don't like the ground rules, don't play.'

'Did I complain? If I wasn't wearing a beak, I'd show you how much I like your rules.'

Rosy blushed and backed off. 'Behave yourself in a public place, Laverton, or I'll have you disqualified.'

'Good thing I'm wearing my beak, then,' he called to her retreating back. He became aware he was being scowled at. 'Hi, Matthew, how's it going?'

'Okay, I s'pose.'

'I hear you're serving drinks at one of the checkpoints.'

'Yeah.' He ground a hole in the gravel with the toe of his sports shoe.

'I might find it a bit hard drinking with my beak. What do you reckon?'

'I reckon you look stupid.' Matthew gave him a long, hard stare that bordered on insolence.

Benedict was momentarily taken aback, but he recovered quickly. 'I think perhaps you're right,' he said evenly, refusing to take offence. 'But my mother got me this costume and I didn't want to disappoint her. You know how sensitive mothers can be.'

Matthew shrugged. 'Guess so.'

'Sometimes we have to do things we're not comfortable with, so we won't hurt the feelings of those we love.'

Matthew ground the gravel deeper.

'So I'm dressed as a bird to please my mum and your mum. And if you laugh at me while I'm trying to run in this rig, then I'll ruffle my feathers at you and peck you with my beak!' said Benedict lightheartedly.

Matt gave a grudging smile. 'It's only

made of foam,' he said before making his way towards the checkpoint.

'And make sure you have a straw in my drink, Matt,' Benedict shouted after him. 'Or I'll use this beak of mine on you!' The boy laughed and waved a hand. Benedict blew out a relieved sigh. Ever since he'd met Rosy Scott, he'd been on a relationship-learning curve and he was sure the curve was going to get curvier the closer he got to his goal.

'Right, we start in two minutes,' said Rosy who was suddenly by his side. 'Everything okay with Matt?'

'Yup, he was just teasing me about my costume.'

'Can't think why. You look so cute.'

'Ms. Scott, you're on dangerous ground.'

'Don't I know it.' Their eyes met for a charged moment.

'You're not the only one, sweetheart. I've been on shifting sands since I met you.'

'Oh, dear, Laverton. Perhaps we should reassess all this?'

'No, I like shifting sands. You're never quite sure what's going to happen.'

'You make it sound dangerous.'

'It is, but it's worth the risk.'

'You scare me.'

'I scare myself.' Benedict looked ruefully at her and was rewarded with a blush.

Yep, those sands shift all the time.

The crack of the starting gun put a stop to further discussion. The runners surged forward, a motley array of pirates, cowboys, fairies, bears, and birds. It wasn't long before the colorful crowd evened out around the oval. In the distance, Benedict could make out Rosy, her jaunty red hearts flapping around her costume. There was no way he could catch up to her. There simply hadn't been enough time to train, though he'd done his best. He followed the other runners as they branched out to jog around the recreation ground and then back to the oval in a big loop which had to be endured several times to clock up the ten kilometers.

On the recreation ground, Benedict passed Josh playing on the playground equipment with some other children from the town. Even though the chicken mask restricted his vision, Benedict recognized a few of the boys from the football team. They all waved to him as he bobbed past, leaving a trail of feathers. Wherever his mother had found the costume, it must have been past its use by date judging by the amount of fluff he was shedding.

At one of the checkpoints, Matt gave him a drink with a straw. Benedict felt a ridiculous amount of pleasure that the boy had listened to him. Perhaps he was finally making progress with him. He hoped so, because there would be no future with Rosy if he didn't have the boys on his side.

He lost count of the number of people who lapped him, but Benedict didn't care. He just wanted to finish the damn run to prove to Rosy he could do it. Sweat blurred his vision, along with his mask. Every so often he unwittingly inhaled a feather. Darn things. Rosy lapped him several times, clapping him on the back as she sailed past with ease.

'Mum's on the last bit,' said Matt, as he handed Benedict another drink. 'I think she might win.'

'Best push on then, so I can see her moment of triumph,' panted Benedict, who had no idea how many more laps he had to endure. He upped his pace, which wasn't easy with flapping claws attached to his joggers, and headed towards the line. He was just in time to see Rosy, arms stretched above her head, break the tickertape. There were cheers and clapping. Benedict felt his chest swell with pride. He increased his speed so he could get close and congratulate her, but suddenly the crowd fell back. Rosy began to sprint through them. What was she doing? Benedict watched in disbelief as Rosy appeared to run a lap of victory. Was the woman crazy? Wasn't ten kilometers enough for anyone to run in one day?

Then, over his labored breathing and

the blood pounding in his head, he became aware that the cheering had stopped. Rosy? Was something the matter with Rosy? Benedict sprinted faster. He heard an ambulance siren. Hell, what had happened? Had she collapsed? Had a stroke? Benedict felt his own blood pressure skyrocket at the thought.

'Hey, mate, what's up?' Benedict asked one of the people in the crowd.

'A kid's been hurt.'

'Where, who?'

'The Scott kid fell off a piece of play equipment.'

Josh! Oh, God, Rosy!

Benedict pushed his way through the milling people. He ran as if his heart would burst until he reached the playground. He caught sight of a torn red heart. Closer, he saw Rosy kneeling on the ground, her Queen of Hearts' crown discarded, forlorn and crumpled at her side. Medics were next to her. Benedict came up behind her and put his arm around her shoulder, which was difficult to accomplish due to his bulbous feathered costume. Rosy, white faced and big eyed, stared at him.

'It's Josh . . . He fell. He's unconscious . . . '

'Hey, honey, it'll be okay. These guys know what they're doing.'

One of the medics glanced up at him. He realized it was the bloke he'd seen in Rosy's waiting room. He looked at the other one. It was the young waiter from the Laughing Duck. 'Are you blokes qualified?' Benedict demanded, panic seizing him.

The waiter said, 'Don't worry, mate. We're trained volunteers. We know basic first aid and, if we hurry, we can get Josh to the hospital in two minutes.' Rosy, who was holding on to Joshua's hand, didn't say anything. 'Rosy, you can come in the ambulance with us,' said the young man.

Rosy did look up then, straight at Benedict. 'Matt,' was all she said.

'I'll find him and bring him to the hospital,' said Benedict. 'Don't worry about a thing. Just concentrate on Josh.'

Benedict swung around. He felt sick to the pit of his stomach. Poor little kid. He hoped Josh would be okay. And Rosy. He wanted to be with her, to support and comfort her. He'd better find Matt quick and get to the hospital.

Fifteen minutes later, Benedict was pacing the waiting room floor. He was still dressed as a chicken. There hadn't been time to change, though he had discarded the head piece. Matt sat on one of the orange plastic seats and stared hard at the door, no doubt willing his mother to come through it and tell him everything was all right. Benedict wished she would too. Instead, Deirdre Bott bustled in.

'It's a serious head injury. It'll be a Royal Flying Doctor's job,' she said without preamble. 'We're getting things ready now. You can have one minute with them before they go.'

Benedict put a comforting hand on Matt's shoulder. Matt shrugged it off and marched through the door, his expression fixed, following Deirdre.

Rosy was still holding Josh's hand. She turned a strained face toward them as they entered the room. Matt rushed to her side where she held him tightly with her free arm. Over his head, she made eye contact with Benedict. She looked lost and desolate. Benedict wished he could take away all her pain and hurt, do anything to make her smile again. But only the doctors could do that by making Josh well. He felt obsolete. The only thing he could do was to be there for her in whatever capacity she needed.

'How is he?' Benedict asked softly.

'Not good.' Her lip trembled and she bit down on it.

Benedict reached out and touched her cheek. 'Hey, sweetheart, Josh is a strong little fella. He'll be fine.'

'I want to go with him to Perth.' She looked at him pleadingly as Matt shoved away Benedict's hand from his mother's face. 'But there's Matt. There's no room in the plane for him.'

'I'll look after Matt. No problem. Isn't that right, mate?' Matt gave him a belligerent scowl that filled Benedict with as much confidence as a stock market crash.

'And what about the animals? Jan's away with the family. I can't think of anybody else on such short notice.' Panic jarred her usually melodic voice.

'Don't worry about a thing, Rosy. We'll take care of everything. You just support young Josh. He needs you. We'll handle things this end. No problem.'

Rosy turned her head to stare back at Josh. 'And we've got to fly!'

Benedict paused a moment, remembering the fear she'd shown during the helicopter ride. He leaned over towards her, ignoring Matt's elbow jabbing in his ribs, and said, 'Honey, you can do it. You managed to fly to Perth safely once and you can do it again. And hey, I shan't be pilot!'

Rosy gave a watery chuckle. 'I suppose I should be thankful for small mercies.'

'Concentrate on Josh. Forget you're

flying. Pretend you're sitting here by his bed and let everyone else do the worrying. Okay?' He gently kissed her cheek as the staff came in to transport Joshua to the ambulance.

★   ★   ★

Ten minutes out of town and the black Jag was already filled with an awful aroma. The chickens weren't house trained and Henry suffered from excess wind due to the excitement of being in a car. Benedict rolled his window down.

'Hey, don't do that, Bert'll get cold and then he'll die and it'll be all your fault,' said Matt.

Benedict silently cursed the parrot as he rolled back up the window. 'The thing is Matt,' said Benedict. 'The smell is really getting to me and we're only a couple of miles out of town. We've a long way to go, son, till Perth.'

'I'm not your son!' Matt's bottom lip jutted out angrily. He crossed his arms tightly across his chest, letting go of

Henry's collar in the process. Henry, who'd been squashed between Matt's feet in the well of the passenger seat, shot up onto the boy's lap and gawked out of the window, tongue lolling.

'Point taken. I'm sorry. It's just an expression. Henry, down!' The dog, pleased at being addressed, leaned over and licked Benedict's cheek. 'Ugh! Down, boy, down! Matt, get that stupid dog down before a cop sees it. We have to open the windows a bit because the smell is rotten. Oh, God, what's wrong with the cat?'

'Moondyke hates cars. He thinks he's going to the vet.'

'Is that a problem?'

'Yup. He's usually sick. Mum hates taking him for his jabs. He makes a gross mess.'

'Great. Anything else I should know?'

'He doesn't like being caged.'

'I think I worked that one out for myself.' Benedict had the scratches to prove it. The cat had fought valiantly not to go into the cat box, while Henry had run crazy circles in the room and hyped everything up by several notches. Brilliant. Perhaps he should have swapped places with Rosy and let her deal with the beasts while he flew. He was beginning to think she had the easier option.

There was a sudden loud commotion with lots of yowling and squawking. Benedict glanced in his rearview mirror. 'What's going on now?'

'Moonie's just realized Zorro is in his cage. He's trying to get him and it's upsetting Bert. He thinks Moonie's after him.'

'Excellent! Perhaps you'd better sit in the back to umpire.'

'What about Henry?' Henry slobbered and wagged his tail with difficulty in the confined space.

'He'll stay on the floor, won't he?' Benedict glanced at Matt who shook his head. 'No?'

'No.'

'No. Right. I think we've got a long journey ahead of us. Let's hope the

goldfish and chickens behave themselves.'
The goldfish were slopping about in the lettuce crisper, the only thing Benedict could find with a close-fitting lid, and the chickens were confined to a large cardboard box with makeshift holes. It was tied with a small piece of wimpy string and Benedict had little confidence in it keeping the birds in if they became flighty. To help anchor it down, he'd put the cat box on top.

The problem was, the Jag wasn't designed as an ark. Benedict realized if he achieved his heart's desire to be part of the Scott household, he'd have to invest in a family size car. The learning curve was still curving.

14

Rosy gazed with unseeing eyes out the high story window of the children's hospital. She didn't register that rain teemed against the glass, traffic-clogged roads were slick and shiny, and streetlights were already on. She'd lost track of the time. The only thing she did know was Josh was in surgery. She bit her knuckle and tried not to let the knot of panic inside her gut unravel. She had to stay calm.

The waiting room was empty except for Rosy. It was painted in bright primary colors. The cheery faces of clowns and cartoon characters failed to raise a smile with Rosy, but she knew Josh would appreciate them. He loved all that fun stuff.

If he came round.

Black panic surged upwards and Rosy fought it back down. Not if, but when. She must have faith.

Her concern hip-hopped to Matt. She hoped he was all right. She hoped Benedict could find someone to mind him. Poor Matt. She wished she could comfort him, but part of her didn't know if she could deal with his needs while little Josh hovered in the half world of unconsciousness. Thank goodness Benedict had been there.

Rosy stiffened.

Benedict.

For the first time in five years, she let a man share her burden. If Janice had been home, she would have automatically enlisted her support. Rosy had no claim on Benedict. And yet, it had been the most natural thing in the world to ask him to care for Matt. She'd known him just three weeks, how could she be so sure she could trust him?

But she did. Implicitly.

Rosy leaned her forehead against the cool window, her breath frosted the glass. Even though the hospital was warm, she felt chilled to the marrow.

She was still in the remnants of her costume. Her legs were bare, her feet still in joggers. She wore only the short Queen of Hearts' dress. She systematically ripped off the last few paper hearts and threw them in a garbage bin. She had no warm clothes to put on. She had no money to buy a coffee or make a phone call. All she had was Josh, lying under a surgeon's knife and Matt miles away at home. She felt rudderless and lost.

She pushed away from the window and aimlessly wandered about the waiting room for the umpteenth time. Finally, she sat on one of the squashy vinyl chairs and picked up a magazine. But she couldn't concentrate on the toothy-smiling Hollywood faces staring out from the pages. She screwed her eyes shut and said yet another prayer for Josh's health. She wrapped her arms around herself and wished it were Benedict's strong arms around her. She suddenly craved him with a need that hurt. The feeling shook her. She was used to being on her own, being strong for her boys. She couldn't expect to rely on Benedict, however much she wanted to.

Resolutely she pulled herself together. She would not fall apart now. Three weeks of knowing him, three nights of loving him did not constitute commitment. Their relationship was for good times. The bad times were for her to contend with as best she could.

She was on her own, again. She shut her eyes and bowed her head to pray for strength.

'Rosy?' Her name shattered the stark silence of the bright room. Rosy's head shot up. She could hardly believe what she saw.

Benedict and Matt.

The boy ran across the room and hurled himself at her. She caught him, kissed him, and hugged him tight.

'Where have you sprung from?' she said, her voice uneven with emotion. She glanced up at Benedict. His figure blurred and shattered into tiny shards as tears rapidly filled her eyes. She blinked them away, dashing her hand across her face.

'Mr. Laverton drove us here in his flash car,' said Matt trying to disentangle himself from his mother's convulsive embrace.

'Goodness.'

'It went really fast.'

'Goodness!' Rosy's eyes narrowed. She stared accusingly at Benedict. The joy of seeing the two of them rapidly abating and was replaced by maternal concern.

'We had to because . . . '

Benedict hurriedly interrupted Matt, 'Because we wanted to get here quickly. Don't panic, sweetheart, I drove carefully and we didn't exceed the speed limit. How's Joshua going?'

Rosy was easily sidetracked. 'He's being operated on,' her voice caught. 'He's been gone ages.'

Benedict reached over the top of Matt's head and cupped her cheek, stroking away a fresh tear. 'He's with the best there is,' he said. 'But if you want a second opinion or another specialist, I can arrange it.'

'Thanks.' His calm solicitude was almost her undoing. Rosy felt her control begin to slip. The panic began to unravel. She quickly clamped down on it. She wouldn't give in to the overwhelming desire to cry her eyes out on Benedict's dependable broad shoulders. Mainly because Matt was there, but also because she knew she would cling to him and need him like she'd needed no other man. It was a frightening admission. She sniffed and swallowed the lump in her throat, again rubbing the back of her hand across her brimming eyes.

She cast about to change the subject. 'Who's looking after the animals?'

Benedict and Matt exchanged a meaningful look. 'They're being taken care of. Don't you worry about a thing,' said Benedict.

Rosy frowned. Something wasn't quite right here. Were they hiding something? 'You would tell me if anything was amiss, wouldn't you?' she said.

'Of course,' said Benedict, whose eyes skittered to Matt again.

'So the animals?'

'Are fine.'

'How come you've got band-aids on your knuckles?'

'It's just a scratch,' said Benedict. 'Now quit worrying. I've brought you a bag of clothes and stuff. I thought you'd like to shower and change into something warm.'

'You packed my clothes?' Rosy had visions of him going through her drawers, of her tatty shirts and threadbare jeans, of her dismal old underwear.

Yet again, she berated herself. She should have acted immediately on Janice's advice and chucked them out, replacing them with new stuff!

Her eyes flew to Benedict's face. He looked sheepish, as if he was embarrassed too.

'Oh, Lord,' she said. 'That was beyond the call of duty.'

'I just grabbed a few things. We were in a hurry. I hope I got what you wanted, but if there's anything else you need just tell me and I'll go and buy it.'

When the moon turned pink! She couldn't have him buy her knickers. She tightened her hold of Matt. 'What about you, darling? Did you pack some gear too?'

'Yeah, Mr. Laverton made me.'

'Good. You behave for him.'

'Can't I stay here with you?'

'I'd love you to, darling. But a hospital is no place for you to hang around. You'd be bored to tears in no time. Mr. Laverton will take care of you tonight.' She looked to Benedict for confirmation.

He nodded and said, 'You're going to stay here then? Not come home with us?'

'I have to. I can't leave Josh.'

'Fine. I'll go and get your clothes from the car and you can change into something more comfortable. Then Matt and I'll go find something to eat.

What about you?'

'I . . . '

'Have you eaten?'

'No. I didn't bring any money with me.' She ridiculously felt like crying again. She was being such a wuss.

Benedict picked up on her distress. He gathered her to him. 'Don't cry, sweetheart. Everything is going to be okay. I'm here to take care of you now. Don't worry about a thing.'

When he was sure she was all right, Benedict went and collected an assortment of plastic Coolumbarup supermarket bags from the Jag. He handed one to Rosy before reaching into another. He pulled out a battered earless teddy bear.

'I thought you might need this, for the little bloke,' said Benedict, an embarrassed twist to his lips. 'You know, I thought it might help him feel a bit more secure.'

Those darn tears gathered at full flood again. Rosy sniffed and snuffled. 'I think you're a star, Benedict Laverton. Josh never sleeps without his bear. He would have been lost without it. And I didn't even think about it.' She sniffled and snuffled some more.

'Hey, don't beat yourself up about it. There wasn't time for you to think of anything but getting Joshua to hospital,' said Benedict. He gave her a tender smile as he tipped her wet face upwards so he could mop her eyes with his handkerchief. 'Between us all, we've done okay. Wouldn't you say, Matt?' he said to the boy, including him in the conversation.

'Yeah, I reckon,' he said and grinned at Benedict as though they had a secret.

'I still think you're holding back on me. You didn't happen to fly here, did you?' she said accusingly.

'Course not and you think too much. I reckon what you need is a hot shower and warm clothes. Go on, be off with you while Matt and I hold the fort and wait for some news of Josh.'

As she let the needles of hot water ease her stiff muscles, Rosy mused on the softer, sensitive side of Benedict.

When she'd first been introduced to him at the bachelor auction, she'd tagged him as a flint-hard businessman, without a heart or conscience, who would put his own interests ahead of anyone else's. But, over the weeks, the layers had peeled away to reveal a kind, caring, generous man who was prepared to put himself out for others.

Take the teddy bear. He had to have raided Joshua's exceedingly untidy bedroom to find it while trying to organize all the other things before leaving for Perth. It was a small act of kindness on his behalf, but a big deal to Josh. He'd be thrilled to have his bear once he awoke.

Rosy sighed. She really liked this man. And then it hit her like a freight train. No, she didn't just like him, she loved him.

Oh Lord. When did that happen?

She shoved the new revelation away. It was much too scary to think about. Especially now with Josh injured. No, she could not even begin to think about it. One thing at a time. Josh was top priority, then a stable family home for the boys. Loving Benedict would have to be relegated to some dark corner of her heart, possibly for ever.

* * *

Early the next morning, Rosy awoke cramped and fuzzy-headed. She'd spent the night curled up in a recliner chair next to Josh's bed, with a scratchy gray hospital blanket thrown over her. Already the ward was like a busy inner-city swap meet. There were so many people — nurses were popping in and out doing blood pressure and temperature checks; cleaners were wiping down all surfaces known to God; kitchen staff were handing out breakfast trays for those lucky enough to be able to eat; and crumpled parents wandered around in a sleep-deprived daze trying to get their act together for another day at their children's bedsides.

Rosy stretched and yawned and then

leaned toward Joshua, gently stroking his hand. He looked so small and diminished in the big steel bed. Like a malnourished angel in thin hospital issue pajamas. Rosy's heart swelled with love for him. He was such a dear little fellow. She hated seeing him swathed in head bandages, his body linked up to tubes and monitors. It was all so alien and clinical. Except, of course, for the moth-eaten teddy bear. She'd tucked it in next to Josh once he'd come out of the recovery ward. Regardless of whether or not Josh felt better about having him there, she certainly did! Bless Benedict.

A little while later, Benedict and Matthew joined her in Joshua's room. Matt wore an interesting combination of patched combat trousers and a too large yellow T-shirt emblazoned with a cartoon character. Rosy didn't deign to say anything about his fashion sense. She wasn't sure if Matt or Benedict had been responsible. At least his hair was brushed.

As for Benedict, Rosy's chest contracted

sharply at the sight of him and then swelled like a balloon with what she now realized was love. He was gorgeous. Darkly handsome in his black jeans and gray cashmere sweater the same shade as his eyes. His black hair was swept back carelessly and he hadn't shaved. She itched to reach out and run her hand over the dark stubble, just to feel the friction under her fingertips. She curled her fingers into fists. Not now, Rosy! She then noticed there was another band-aid on his hand — his other hand, this time. But before Rosy could ask about it, the doctor came in.

'Mr. and Mrs. Scott,' said the doctor. 'About Joshua.'

Rosy nervously rose to her feet, 'Actually,' she said. 'We're not-'

Benedict draped a reassuring arm around Rosy's shoulders and pulled her close to his side. 'We're all ears, doctor,' he said, not correcting the doctor's mistake.

'But!' said Rosy. Benedict's hand slipped down her back. His thumb snagged in the top of her back pocket and his fingers and palm comfortably cupped her right buttock. 'Oh,' she said and was effectively silenced.

'Good news,' the doctor informed them. 'The operation seems to have been successful. We've managed to relieve the pressure on the brain. Once the swelling goes down, and we're sure there are no infections or complications, we can send him to your local hospital to recuperate. We're confident Joshua will be fit as a fiddle in no time at all. He's a tough little lad.'

Rosy couldn't remember what was said during the next few moments. She let Benedict do the talking while she turned into the hard heat of his chest and quietly cried tears of relief. His arm was a firm band around her. She felt secure and cared for. She tuned in and out of the conversation.

' . . . so he'll remain in this ward for the next few days . . . keep him quiet . . . happy for someone to be with him at all times . . . '

'I don't care how long we have to be here,' Rosy said after the doctor had gone. 'As long as Josh is going to be okay.'

'And he will be. You heard the doctor.' Benedict hugged her close. 'Everything's going to be fine, Rosy.'

The day dragged by. Benedict insisted Rosy take some time out with Matthew while he stayed by Joshua's bedside. Rosy and Matt bought chicken and salad rolls from the hospital café and took them to eat at the nearby park, throwing crumbs to the birds. It was good to feel the cold damp air on their faces after the constant air conditioning of the hospital, to stretch their legs, and let the wind ruffle their hair. Once again, by the time the tea trays were being delivered, Benedict and Matthew said their goodbyes and left Rosy with Josh.

It wasn't a good night. Josh was no longer unconscious and began to fret about staying still in bed. He wanted food, he wanted to play, he didn't want to sleep and he really, really didn't want the tubes sticking into him and the hot bandages on his head. Rosy endlessly read stories to him to keep him occupied until he once again slipped off to sleep. She was exhausted and wished Benedict was there with her. She missed him terribly.

Josh woke several times during the night and by morning, Rosy was hanging out for Benedict's arrival so he could share the load with Josh, except it wasn't him walking into the room with Matt. It was Hovea in a navy blue power suit and high heels.

'Darling,' said Hovea, while watching Rosy hugging and kissing Matt. 'Good to see you again, though not in these terrible circumstances.' She did an expressive gesture towards Josh. 'Poor little mite. Too awful.'

'He's getting much better,' said Rosy. 'The worst is hopefully over.'

'Excellent. Look, I hope you don't mind me being here, but Benedict asked if I could bring Matthew in on my way to the office.'

Yes, Rosy did mind. Dreadfully. She wanted Benedict.

Instead she said, 'No, I'm grateful you could do it. What's happen to Benedict? Caught up with his business?'

She hoped she didn't sound too disappointed or too nosy. Benedict didn't have to visit the hospital every single day. He wasn't duty bound to do so. Josh wasn't his child. As it was, he was doing a marvelous job taking care of Matt. Anyway, Benedict had plenty of other commitments. Really, if Rosy was honest with herself, the Scott family and its problems didn't require a Benedict Laverton commitment. Rosy had to remember that, in spite of her love for Benedict. Their relationship wasn't a firm one. It was based on attraction and who knew how long that would last, now that Benedict had been given a huge dose of how complicated life could be with a woman with a ready made family. He was probably already distancing himself and she couldn't blame him one bit. As she'd said a few days ago, men balked at becoming involved with a single mother.

'Not business exactly,' said Hovea, glancing at Matt and then back to Rosy. 'But he is terribly busy. He said to give you his love and he'd be with you as soon as he's finished.' She glanced at Matt again. Matt grinned and so did Hovea.

Rosy bristled suspiciously. But before she could ask them exactly what Benedict had to finish, Hovea was kissing her cheek, patting Matt on the head, and saying she was late for the office. Rosy turned to Matt. 'Okay,' she said, 'what's going on?'

'Nothing.'

'I don't believe you.'

'Mr. Laverton has got a brilliant pool. He said I could swim in it if it was okay with you.'

'Your bathers are at home.'

'He said he'd buy me some.'

'And it's winter.'

'The pool's heated.'

'No problem then, as long as there's

an adult with you all the time.'

'Thanks, Mum. I think I'll find a book to read until Josh wakes up,' said Matt innocently and disappeared out of the room toward the communal book-shelves. Rosy stared after him. She'd been had, and by a seven-year-old. Perhaps proximity to Benedict was teaching him bad habits!

When Benedict did eventually turn up, it was around lunchtime. There was another day's growth on his chin. His blue jeans were grass stained. He wore a dark green cable knit sweater. He looked sexy, rumpled, and wounded.

'You're limping,' said Rosy as he hobbled towards her.

'Not me.' He kissed her on the top of the head, then on the tip of her nose, and finally her mouth. 'Missed you,' he said. 'How are things going with Josh?'

'I've missed you too,' said Rosy, suddenly feeling all warm and mushy inside. 'Josh is getting demanding.'

'He must be feeling better then. Where's Matt?'

'Reading and avoiding me.'

'Why?'

'Because I asked some questions he didn't want to answer.'

'Oh.' The tone, Rosy noticed, was carefully non-committal.

'And here's one for you. How did you get the scratch on your nose?' Rosy asked as she pulled him back down for another kiss. As she surfaced for air, Rosy stroked back a lock of Benedict's black hair. 'And you've grazed your temple. How did you do that?'

'That's two questions. I think I'll go and join Matt.'

'Oh, no you don't!' Rosy grabbed a handful of green jumper. 'Spill the beans, Laverton.' She let go as Matt came in the room and said to him, 'Do you know anything about Benedict's war wounds, Matthew?'

'I didn't do it,' he said indignantly.

'I never said you did, but you do know how he did it?'

Matt's expression flickered. His eyes slid to Benedict.

'Matt,' said Rosy, sounding as though she meant business.

Matt sighed. 'Moonie did the scratches.'

'Moondyke! That soft old thing!'

Benedict snorted. 'Nothing soft about that feline monster.'

'Hold on a moment,' said Rosy, frowning. 'That's a fresh scratch.'

Benedict fingered his wounded nose. 'Couldn't get much fresher.'

'But Moondyke is at home in Coolumbarup. Left there a couple of days ago, or so I believed.'

Benedict and Matt exchanged a guilty look.

'By your silence, I guess that's not the case,' she said mildly.

Matt was the first to crack. He shook his head.

'So where is he?'

'At Mr. Laverton's house.'

'And Henry?'

'He's there too.'

Rosy's lips twitched. 'What about the other animals?'

'They're all there.'

362

'Even the chickens?' Rosy regarded Benedict in astounded fascination. He nodded. 'Oh, my. When I asked you to take care of things, I didn't mean to burden you with a bunch of fur and feather. I thought you'd ask the neighbors to do it.'

'I didn't know your neighbors and Jan was away, so I decided to ship them all here so we could keep an eye on them.'

'How?'

'In the Jag,' volunteered Matt. 'It was gross.'

Rosy began to giggle. 'Oh, Benedict. How have you housed them all?'

'Moondyke is being kept inside so he wouldn't get lost. He doesn't like it and keeps trying to escape every time a door is opened.'

'Hence the scratches.'

'Yes, hence the scratches. It's not funny, Ms. Scott, that cat is dangerous with a capital D.'

'And the limp?'

'Henry.'

'You're kidding?'

'I was standing on the ladder, tacking the last of the wire to the gazebo, when he decided to chase the neighbor's Persian cat. He collected the ladder as he went by.'

Rosy's eyes danced merrily. 'I probably shouldn't ask this, but why the wire on the gazebo?'

'You're right, you shouldn't ask.'

Rosy laughed at Benedict's long suffering expression.

There was movement in the bed. 'Hello, mate,' said Benedict to Joshua, who was just waking up from a nap. 'How are you going?'

'Okay. Why are you all laughing? What's so funny?'

'Moonie scratched Mr. Laverton and Henry knocked him off the ladder,' said Matthew.

'That's not funny,' said Josh and rolled over and went back to sleep.

'I love that kid. He's smart,' said Benedict.

'You mean he's temporarily lost his

sense of humor,' grinned Rosy.

That evening, Rosy felt confident enough to leave Joshua at the hospital so she could have a decent night's sleep in a bed. Nights of catnapping in the reclining chair were taking their toll and she was exhausted. Benedict drove them through the endless evening traffic to the quiet, luxurious suburb where he had his home. Rosy gasped when she saw the honey-brick Federation mansion. It had a huge lush garden of palms and ferns overlooking the Swan River

'You live here?'

'Yes, ma'am.'

'But it's gorgeous!'

'I don't know whether to feel flattered by the obvious surprise in your voice or not,' said Benedict as he swung the black Jaguar through the wrought iron gates and up the graveled driveway. 'What did you expect me to live in? No, don't tell me. Let me guess. A modern high rise penthouse with black and gray steel furniture and a massive abstract painting in the foyer.'

'Something like that.'

'Sorry to disappoint you, but I gave up that sort of thing years ago.'

'You haven't disappointed me.'

Benedict slanted her a toe-curling smile. 'Good. I hoped you'd approve.'

'As if that matters.'

'It does. Believe me.' The air shimmered between them with sudden electricity.

'Mum, wait until you see the pool. It's great,' said Matthew, successfully breaking the heated tension.

'I'm sure,' said Rosy, letting Matt pull her out of the car and up the wide sweep of stone steps to the stained-glass front door. 'You can show me all of it.'

The house was as beautiful inside as out, though rather untidy. Rosy spotted at least one of Matthew's socks discarded on the floor. She automatically picked it up.

'Sorry about the mess,' said Benedict over the din of Henry's rapturous welcome. 'But my housekeeper is on her annual holiday and I haven't had much time to do anything.'

'Because of us. Let me tell you now, I'm used to mess in a big way. It's called living with children. This is all so beautiful, Benedict.' Rosy ran her hands over a polished antique table on which a glossy leafed aspidistra had pride of place in a fine china bowl. 'It's absolutely fantastic.'

And not a jot like her place, with its serviceable Formica table and hotch-potch cheap furniture.

'Come and see the pool!'

'I'm coming, Matt. Get down, Henry.'

As they approached the sunken pool, Henry ran ahead of them and then took a spectacular dive in the deep end.

'Henry!' yelled Benedict. 'Get out of there!' The dog ignored him and happily doggy paddled to the shallow end. Benedict heaved him out by the scruff of his neck. 'Damn dog.' With that, the damn dog shook himself, saturating Benedict. 'Great! Just great.'

Matthew was doubled over with laughter. 'Henry does that every night, Mum. Without fail.'

'Oh, dear,' said Rosy and meant it. Then she spotted the gazebo. It had jasmine and bougainvillea twining around its latticework.

And lots of new chicken wire inexpertly attached to the structure.

Rosy frowned and made her way over the manicured lawn to the pavilion-style gazebo. She peered through the wire and saw her chickens cozily perched inside.

'Nice chicken house, Laverton. Rather posh.'

'Top of the range.'

'Though a bit extreme, I'd say, for a bunch of old chooks.'

'Couldn't think of anywhere else to put them and I drew the line at the laundry. A feline fiend and a mountain of cat litter is enough in there.'

'Poor Benedict.'

'You can make it up to me later,' he waggled his eyebrows and Rosy felt her cheeks heating and her insides melting at the idea of 'later'.

'It's a tough life,' she said with a grin.

Back inside, Benedict asked Matthew to show his mother the spare bedroom so she could freshen up. 'Why don't you have a long hot soak in the bath while I organize dinner,' he said. 'I brought you a few extra clothes which are already in your room. I thought you might need them.'

In her bedroom, Rosy fingered the new clothes laid out on the queen-size bed. There were soft lambs wool jumpers in peach, light blue, and primrose yellow, black linen slacks, an emerald green skirt, a couple of cotton blouses, and a pale lilac silk nightdress with matching dressing gown. Rosy blew out the air from her cheeks. Goodness. She'd never owned so many new clothes. How could she accept them?

She ran her fingers over the silk again and then a gleam came into her eye. It'd be a shame to waste it.

The first bathroom she entered was already in use and so she opted for the one near the master bedroom. She filled the bathtub with bubble bath and enjoyed a delicious hot soak. She washed and rinsed her hair under the shower and then toweled herself dry. She looked at the swathe of lilac silk draped over the bathroom chair. Should she? Could she? A smile flickered around her lips. You betcha! 'That's pretty, Mum,' said Matthew when Rosy, rather self-consciously, made her way to the kitchen a little while later.

'It is, isn't it,' said Rosy, giving a twirl so the silk blew out around her and resettled on her slightly damp curves.

Benedict turned around from the stove where he was grilling steaks. His eyes became hot silver pools as they alighted on those curves in the form fitting silk. 'Very pretty,' he said.

'Steaks are burning, Laverton,' said Rosy sweetly.

'Not the only thing,' he replied before dragging the grill pan from the flame.

'By the way, I love the goldfish swimming in the bath tub. I'm not up on these things, but it must be the latest innovation in interior decor,' said Rosy, wandering around the kitchen touching the gleaming black marble surfaces with the tips of her fingers, running her palm over the rich red jarrah cupboards. 'I had to use your bathroom. I hope you don't mind.'

'Not at all. Make yourself at home. Those fish don't have a decorative function, or any function, as far as I can see. They're your fish. I couldn't think where else to keep them,' explained Benedict.

Rosy chuckled. 'I know. I recognized them.'

'Lady, you never cease to amaze me. How on earth can you tell if they're your fish or not?'

'They're part of the family. Of course I recognize them. And they all have names.'

'Spare me. I don't need to know them. I don't have that sort of relationship with them. Now, the steaks are well and truly ready. Salad is in the fridge and the Merlot is open. Care for a glass?'

Rosy opened the fridge. The light didn't automatically come on, so she depressed the light switch a couple of times then shrugged and took out the salad and put the bowl on the kitchen table. She then picked up her full wine glass and wandered over to the birdcage. 'Oh dear, Bert isn't looking too good,' she said.

'His feathers began falling out during the car ride. It must have been all the excitement and that damn cat,' said Benedict.

'Hello, Bert,' said Rosy.

'Damn cat,' said the bird. 'Damn dog.'

'Oh dear,' said Rosy. 'I wonder where he learned to say that?' She raised her brows at Benedict, her eyes dancing.

'No idea,' he said. 'Maybe the mailman. Now let's eat.'

During the meal, Matthew confessed

to Rosy the rat had escaped. 'We can't find him anywhere,' he said. 'And I'm worried Moonie will find him and eat him.' His bottom lip wobbled and he blinked rapidly.

'Hey, don't worry about it, sweetheart. We'll find him.'

'We will?' Matt and Benedict said in unison, one hopeful and the other skeptical.

'Of course,' she said confidently and thought instantly of how the fridge light didn't work and yet everything else seemed to be in good working order in Benedict's palatial home. 'I think I know exactly where he is,' she said. 'I'll show you after dinner.'

'How did you know,' asked Benedict, as he pushed the fridge back toward the wall a while later.

'When you've lived with children and animals as long as I have, you get to know these things,' said Rosy with a grin.

'Good thing I'm a fast learner,' said Benedict.

What am I meant to make of that? She wasn't sure, but it gave her a nice warm glow. Maybe she'd find out later.

She drained her wine and told Matthew it was time for bed. She tucked him in, read a story, and then returned to the kitchen where Benedict had cleared the dinner debris.

'If it's all the same to you, I'll turn in,' said Rosy. She was standing in the doorway in her clingy silk and couldn't help but smile when Benedict huskily said he didn't mind at all and he'd join her as soon as he'd fed the dog and showered.

Rosy almost walked on air back to her bedroom. This was going to be one good night, but she hadn't been in bed two minutes before Matthew came padding in barefoot.

'Can I have a cuddle,' he said.

'Of course, sweetheart.' Rosy pulled up the sheets so he could snuggle in with her. He tucked in close and after chattering for a while he began to get drowsy.

'You know, Mum,' he said, just before falling asleep. 'I like Mr. Laverton. He's cool.'

'I'm glad you like him, Matt. I like him too. Very much.'

★　★　★

After seeing Rosy in her shimmering silk, Benedict went into overdrive. He raced out to feed Henry and then marched him around the garden a few times for a spot of relief before shutting him in the kitchen. He fed the cat, decided to leave the litter changing until the morning, and then dove into the shower. The bathroom smelled of woman, of Rosy. Of her strawberry shampoo and the fresh scent that seemed to be hers alone. It was intoxicating. It was sexy.

In double quick time, he'd showered and shaved and now, with just a towel around his hips and his hair still damp, he tiptoed to her room. It was dark and quiet.

And there was one too many in the bed.

Darn!

But cute.

But darn all the same.

Rosy and Matthew were snuggled together in the big bed, fast asleep. It was a crushing downer for Benedict's charged body. He couldn't help but feel moved by the sight of the boy cocooned in his mother's embrace. Okay, so he would rather it was his head nestled against the swell of Rosy's breast, and his breath mingling with her sweet breath, and his arm flung casually around her soft scented neck. But hell, this was the next best thing.

At least she was in his home, sleeping in one of his beds, and wearing the clothes he'd bought for her.

It was only a matter of time before she'd be in his bed and not wearing *anything*.

Except perhaps, a ring.

15

Sunlight spilled through the thin wooden slats of the blinds, criss-crossing the rumpled bed and disturbing the sleeping woman. Rosy rolled away from the bothersome light and snuggled deeper under the goose feather duvet, trying to recapture the shades of sleep. But it was too late. She was awake now.

After a while, she became aware of the low thuds of a ball landing against a brick wall and the high pitched barking of a dog. Sighing, she squinted at the clock on the bedside table. Goodness, it was eight already. Why hadn't Benedict woken her? Or Matthew, for that matter.

She stretched lazily, flexing her bare arms above her head and then relaxed. She should really get up and check on Josh. It was only his second day away from the hospital. But this was too delicious for words, lounging in bed with no pressing troubles, knowing there was someone else to fix breakfast.

Rosy grinned to herself. She was growing soft. She couldn't remember the last Saturday morning she'd lain abed. Of course, she blamed it on Benedict. He'd spoiled her rotten these past few weeks, while Josh had been recuperating in hospital. Her smile slipped slightly as she wondered what would happen now, now that her son was well enough to go home to Coolumbarup. Would things continue with Benedict? Would he still make the effort to come and see her? They hadn't discussed the changes in their relationship. They'd just let things drift along naturally.

It wasn't that she'd avoided the subject. She'd just been too busy with her daily commute to the hospital, making sure Matt did the homework sent by his school, and trying to minimize the impact of the Scott family and its animals on Benedict's pristine home.

Okay, so there had been ample time in the evenings, when she and Benedict had enjoyed a glass of wine over their meal and discussed the day's events like an old married couple.

But she hadn't wanted to spoil those magical evenings trying to define their relationship.

She knew he cared and it was understandable they had grown closer during their weeks together. But perhaps she was reading too much into things, relying too heavily on the mirage created by their forced proximity. Maybe he was just being too kind to rebuff her.

Noise outside her bedroom door made her shunt the uncomfortable thought away.

There was a brief knock.

'May we come in?' asked Benedict, poking his head around the door.

'Of course, the more the merrier.'

'Good.' Benedict strode in carrying Josh in his arms and plonked him on the bed next to Rosy.

'Morning, Mummy,' he said. His cold little feet scrabbled down her leg as he wriggled close to her, burrowing under the covers.

'Morning, sweetheart. How are you feeling?'

'Pretty good.'

'Excellent. And what about you two? I heard the football earlier.'

'Yeah, Ben and me thought we'd do some training so we don't get out of shape,' said Matthew.

'Not much chance of that,' grinned Rosy, casting a suggestive eye over Benedict's slightly damp T-shirt. It was stuck delectably to his broad, muscular chest. A chest she had run her hands over only a few hours ago when they'd made love.

'Oh, I don't know,' said Benedict. 'All these home cooked meals I'm eating are spoiling me.'

'Oh dear. Perhaps they'd better stop.' Rosy nibbled her bottom lip, wondering if he was giving subtle hints he wanted her out of his home.

'No can do. I'd suffer withdrawal symptoms. No, sorry lady, I think you're stuck with the job. Don't think I can function without you. What do you reckon, boys?'

'I think it's time for breakfast,' said Matt. 'I thought we were having it in Mum's bed?'

'Too right you are. It's all ready to go. I shan't be a tick.' Benedict brushed a kiss over Rosy's cheek and left the room.

Matt frowned. Uh-oh, what was troubling him? He hadn't got worried over Benedict's casual kisses for a while. Rosy waited a second and then prompted him.

'What's up, Matt?'

'Ben said you're stuck with the job of cooking the meals.'

'Yes?' She wondered where this was leading.

'But he takes turns cooking as well,' said Matt.

'What I meant,' said Benedict, as he re-entered the room bearing a tray piled high with buttered toast and tea. 'Is that I think you should all hang around for a long while yet. I don't think there's any rush for you to go back to Coolumbarup. What do you say?'

He addressed the question to Matt, but his eyes zeroed on Rosy's and held her gaze with the warmth of his own.

That warmth penetrated every single atom of her body and made her glow. He wanted her to stay a while. That was good enough for her. She would stay as long as he wanted her too.

'Cool,' said Matt.

'Yeah, great,' said Joshua, emerging from the depths of the duvet. 'Then I can have a swim in the pool too.'

'Brilliant,' said Rosy, her eyes twinkling. 'Now where's the tea and toast. I'm hungry.'

'You're an insatiable woman,' grinned Benedict who, Rosy was sure, looked just as relieved and happy as she felt.

★　★　★

Benedict couldn't believe he'd been suckered again. What was it about his mother and bachelor auctions? Perhaps she should bid for her own man and then she wouldn't be so hell-bent to match everybody else up with a partner.

Especially him.

Okay, so he knew it was all for a good cause, though he couldn't quite remember what it was. Something for a baby unit? Or was it for overseas war refugees? The actual cause eluded him for the moment and it didn't matter a jot, because he wanted to be with Rosy and here he was stuck with a ballroom full of shrilly squawking women. He couldn't make out what they were saying, but their brightly painted mouths opened and shut like Rosy's pet goldfish that had recently been moved out of the bath and into a new aquarium.

He'd tried his hardest to persuade Rosy to attend this charity dance with him, but she'd categorically stated she was allergic to bachelor auctions.

Huh! She was allergic and she wasn't

even the one for sale! Once again, he was being auctioned for a fist full of dollars and he didn't know it until he'd arrived at the function. It made him suspicious Rosy had insider trading details from his wretched mother. Rosy obviously didn't want to cramp Martha's so-called style.

He tugged at his collar. It felt like a noose, a tight noose. Which rich woman would win the dubious honor of his company? This time it wasn't for a mere dinner. Oh no. It was for a whole weekend — their choice of time and place. He had no say in the matter. How awful.

The charity auction was being held in one of the top Perth hotels and attended by the city's elite. His mother anticipated serious money would be raised by the event. He was pleased for her, but at what price to him? Benedict hated being served up like a slab of meat. It made him extremely uncomfortable.

This time there was no sweet Rosy to

bail him out. Damn.

He just wished his mother had told him about the auction earlier. Like before, she'd volunteered him and as before she'd gotten him to escort her.

This was becoming too much of a habit. He had told Martha quite plainly; this was the very last time he'd agree to be auctioned. He hadn't liked the twinkle in her eye, but she hadn't argued with him. With that, he had to be content.

The problem was he really didn't want to spend time with any woman but Rosy. The idea of a weekend wining and dining anybody else was repugnant.

He only wanted Rosy. Dear, gorgeous, zany Rosy with all her wit and exuberance. His mind dwelt, as it often did these days, on her. She'd be at home. He glanced at his Rolex. And the boys would be in bed. She'd probably be curled up on the sofa with a glass of white wine watching the television. Or in bed reading, her glasses perched provocatively on the tip of her nose. He

wished he were in bed with her. And
they wouldn't be reading . . .

'Do I have a bid?' said the auctioneer.

Benedict was thankful he wasn't the
first cab off the rank. Some other poor
bloke had drawn the short straw. But by
the time it was Benedict's turn, he was
feeling decidedly belligerent. One look
at his scowling face should have put the
women off, but the bidding was brisk.
Benedict was sweating buckets in his
tux. He hoped some rich, sweet old
lady would take mercy on him. He
didn't expect it to be his mother.

The bids spiraled. Benedict couldn't
tell who was doing the bidding. The
stage spotlight blinded him. He could
only make out the gawking faces at
the front tables. It wasn't comforting.
Hungry piranhas sprang to mind.

'Two thousand. Do I have another
bid?' said the auctioneer.

'Three!' A low, husky voice floated
from somewhere at the back of the hall.
Heads bobbed about to see who'd
made the bid.

Benedict strained to see too. An explosion of adrenaline coursed through him. Surely he was hearing things, but the voice sounded very familiar.

'Any advance on three?' said the auctioneer.

'Four,' said a confident, cut-glass voice from another part of the hall.

'Five,' said the low, husky voice that held more than a hint of laughter.

Benedict grinned. Suddenly he was enjoying himself. The weekend deal didn't seem like such a terrifying ordeal after all. In fact, he had plans and he hoped she did too.

'Six,' said cut-glass.

'Ten thousand,' said Rosy decidedly, as if defying anyone else to bid.

Benedict's grin widened. That's my girl!

There was a murmur of surprised admiration from the crowd. Benedict fleetingly wondered who'd be doing the paying. Not that he cared. He'd pay the earth for his darling Rosy.

'Do I have another bid?' Silence.

'Any other bids?' Dead silence. 'Ten, going once, going twice, going three times. Congratulations to the lady at the back of the hall. Would you please come forward so we can get your particulars?'

There was rousing applause as Rosy, wearing a ruby-red dress, with her hair swept up in a sophisticated chignon, sashayed towards the stage with more than a hint of a wiggle. Her eyes were on Benedict. A wide, Cheshire cat smile played across her face.

Benedict held out his hand to her and helped her onto the stage before pulling her into a deep, breath-taking kiss.

'I think we're getting the hang of this,' said Rosy when he finally released her. 'Though I do think you're meant to wait for the MC to say when you can kiss me.'

'I couldn't wait, sweetheart. You look divine.' His voice was full of husky emotion.

'You're only pleased to see me because

I saved your skin again,' giggled Rosy.

'Excuse me,' said an official looking person, who was awkwardly standing next to them, 'but can we get your payment details, madam.'

'Of course,' said Rosy, tucking her arm into the crook of Benedict's and following the woman to the edge of the stage.

'How are you going to pay?' said the official.

'Ah,' said Rosy. She glanced up through her thick lashes at Benedict. 'That could be a slight problem.' She unlaced her arm from Benedict and, with both her hands, patted them down the expanse of her slinky dress, knowing full well it would get Benedict's complete attention. 'I seem to have left my purse at home.'

'You can't pay? Have you been wasting our time?' said the official with a disapproving frown.

Benedict gave a rueful laugh. 'Rosy, you are a terrible tease! I'll write a check now,' he said to the woman.

'No negotiations this time?' quipped Rosy.

'No. I'm yours to command for the weekend. Now let's get this paperwork done.'

Once it was completed, Benedict said, 'You know, Rosy. I don't think I can afford any more of these bachelor gigs. It's costing me a small fortune.'

'You'll have to be firm with your mother, then, because she's incorrigible.'

'I've got a better solution.'

'What's that?'

Benedict drew her toward him, encircling her within his arms, and nuzzling her sweet smelling neck. He trailed kisses up to her ear, where he nibbled on her delicate lobe, and then skimmed his lips over her cheek until they hovered over her saucily curving mouth. Benedict felt her body responding to his and he held her tighter.

'Well, Ms. Scott,' he said. 'I see it this way. The only way to stop being a bachelor is to get married. To get married, I need a woman, and there's only one woman I want to marry. That's you. So, what do you say?'

He felt her go still, incredibly still, and his heart squeezed in desperation. Suddenly, he wasn't so sure of her. Suddenly, he doubted all they'd shared these past few weeks wouldn't count for anything. He chastised himself, that he'd moved too quickly, that she needed more time to know they were right together. But he didn't want to wait any longer — couldn't. He wanted her more than anything else in the world.

Say yes, he urged silently, say yes!

Rosy pulled back slightly. She gave him a level look. 'What's your bid, Laverton?' she said. Her voice trembled slightly.

'My love,' he said huskily. 'My life.'

'Done,' she said and gave him a brilliant smile. 'And now you can claim your prize.'

THE END